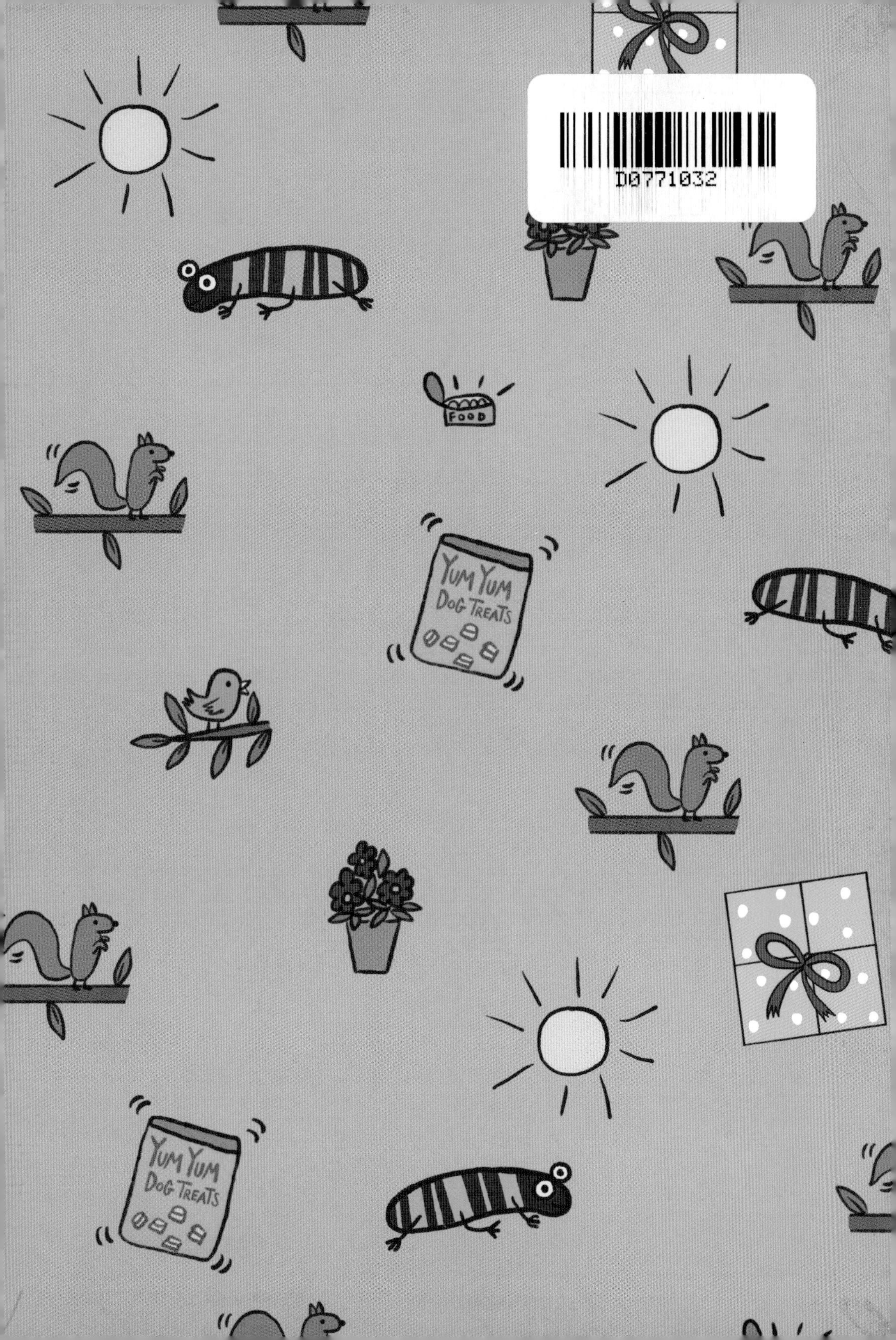
FOOD
YUM YUM
DOG TREATS
YUM YUM
DOG TREATS

About This Book

The text was set in Colby; hand-lettering by Charise Mericle Harper.

· Little, Brown and Company · Hachette Book Group · 1290 Avenue of the Americas, New York, NY 10104 · Visit us at LBYR.com · First Edition: February 2023 Little, Brown and Company is a division of Hachette Book Group, Inc. · The Little, Brown name and logo are trademarks of Hachette Book Group, Inc. · The publisher is not responsible for websites (or their content) that are not owned by the publisher. · Library of Congress Cataloging-in-Publication Data Names: Harper, Charise Mericle, author, illustrator. · Title: Pepper & Boo : paws up for joy! / by Charise Mericle Harper. · Other titles: Pepper and Boo · Description: First edition. | New York ; Boston : Little, Brown and Company, 2023. | Series: Pepper & Boo ; 3 | Audience: Ages 6–10. | Summary: "Pepper, Boo, and the Cat celebrate a special day with big and small things, cat and dog things, as well as inside and outside things." —Provided by publisher. · Identifiers: LCCN 2021053745 | ISBN 9780759555099 Subjects: CYAC: Dogs—Fiction. | Cats—Fiction. | Happiness—Fiction. | LCGFT: Picture books · Classification: LCC PZ7.H231323 Pd 2023 | DDC [E]—dc23 · LC record available at https://lccn.loc.gov/2021053745 · ISBN 978-0-7595-5509-9 PRINTED IN CHINA · APS · 10 9 8 7 6 5 4 3 2 1

PEPPER & BOO

PAWS UP FOR JOY!

(NOT BOO)

by Charise Mericle Harper

L B

Little, Brown and Company
New York Boston

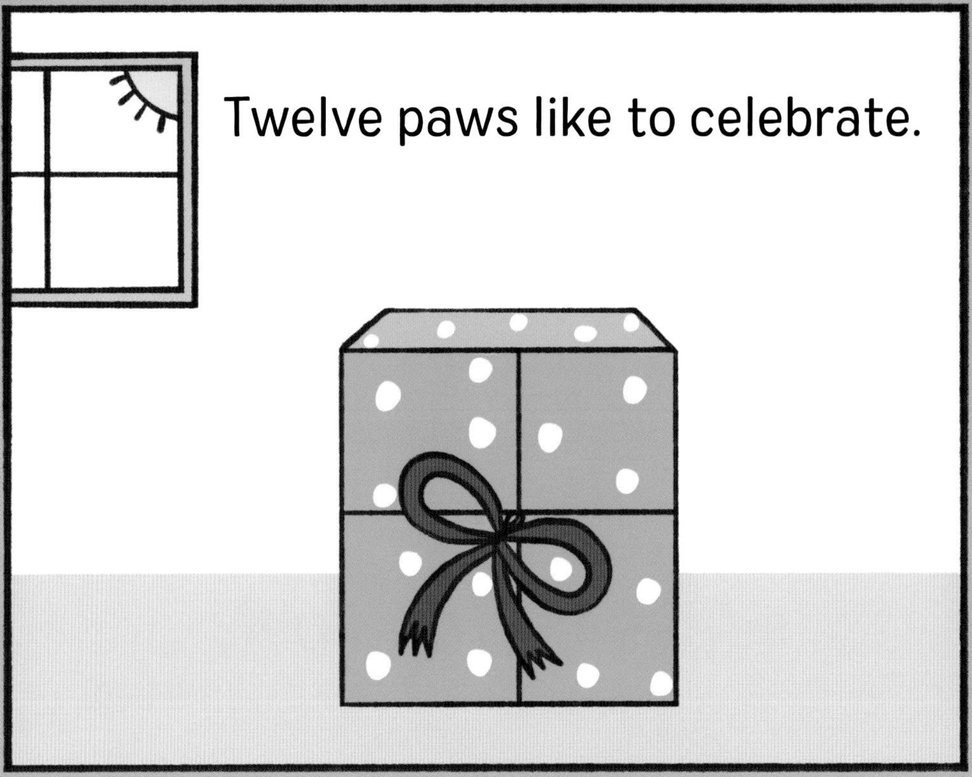
Twelve paws like to celebrate.

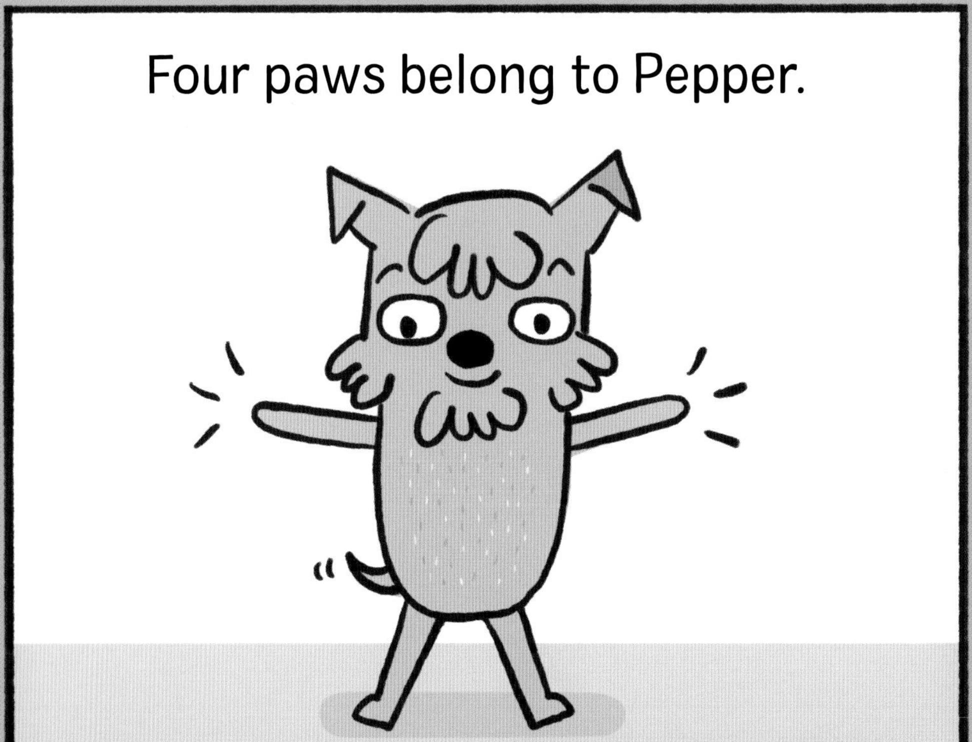
Four paws belong to Pepper.

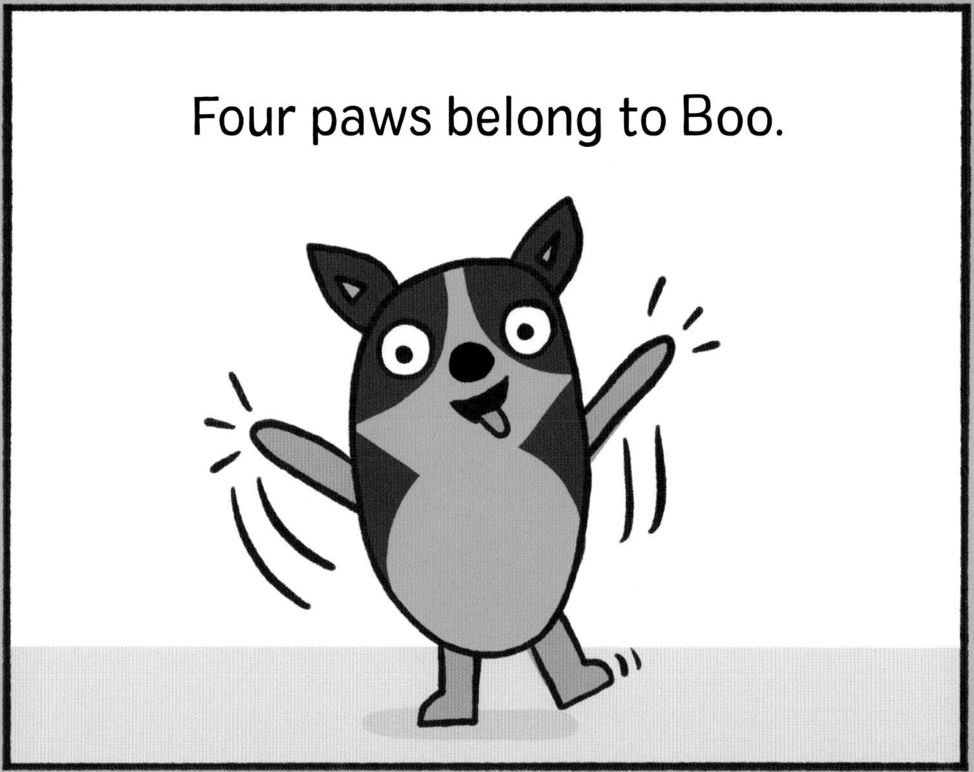
Four paws belong to Boo.

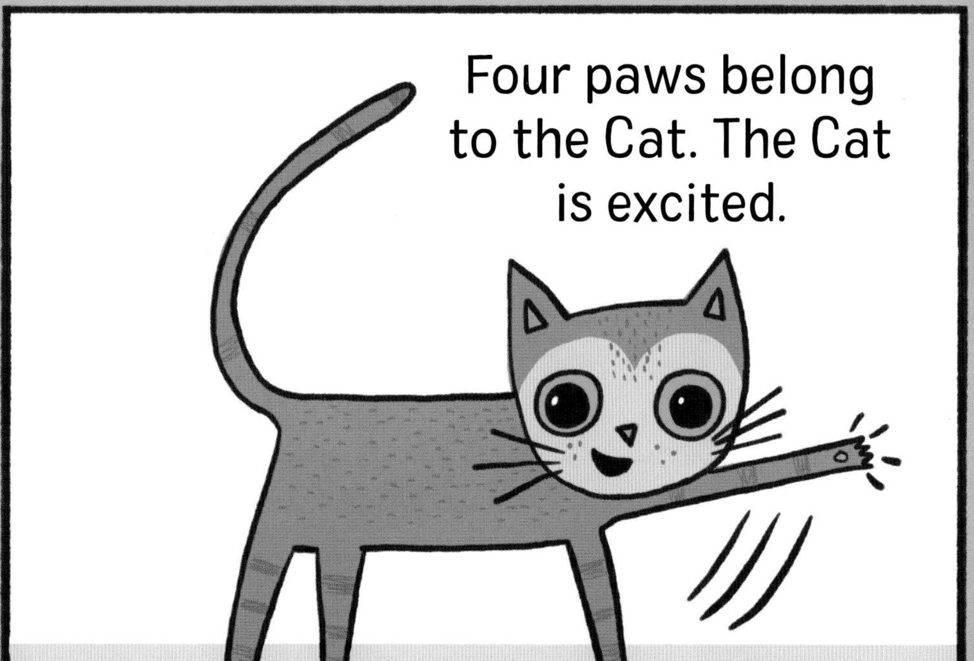
Four paws belong to the Cat. The Cat is excited.

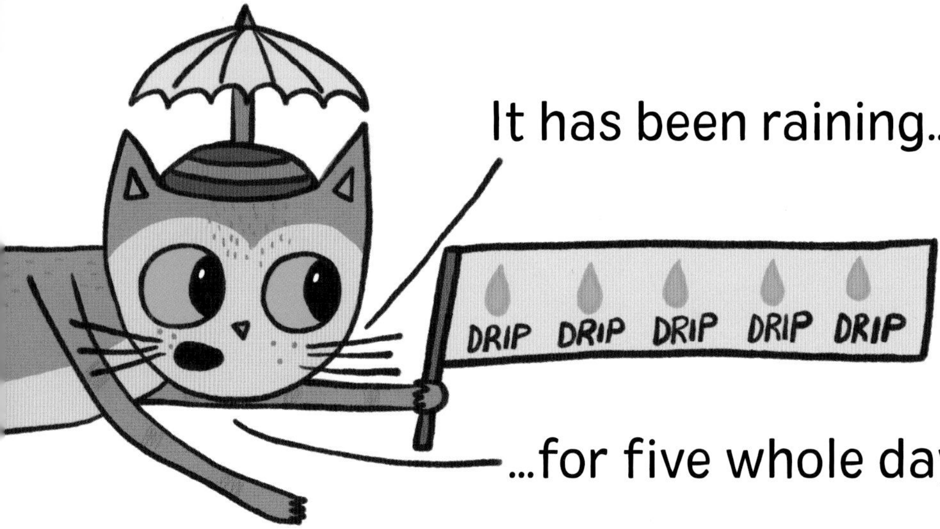
DRIP DRIP DRIP DRIP DRIP

It has been raining...

...for five whole days.

But today,
the sun is
shining!

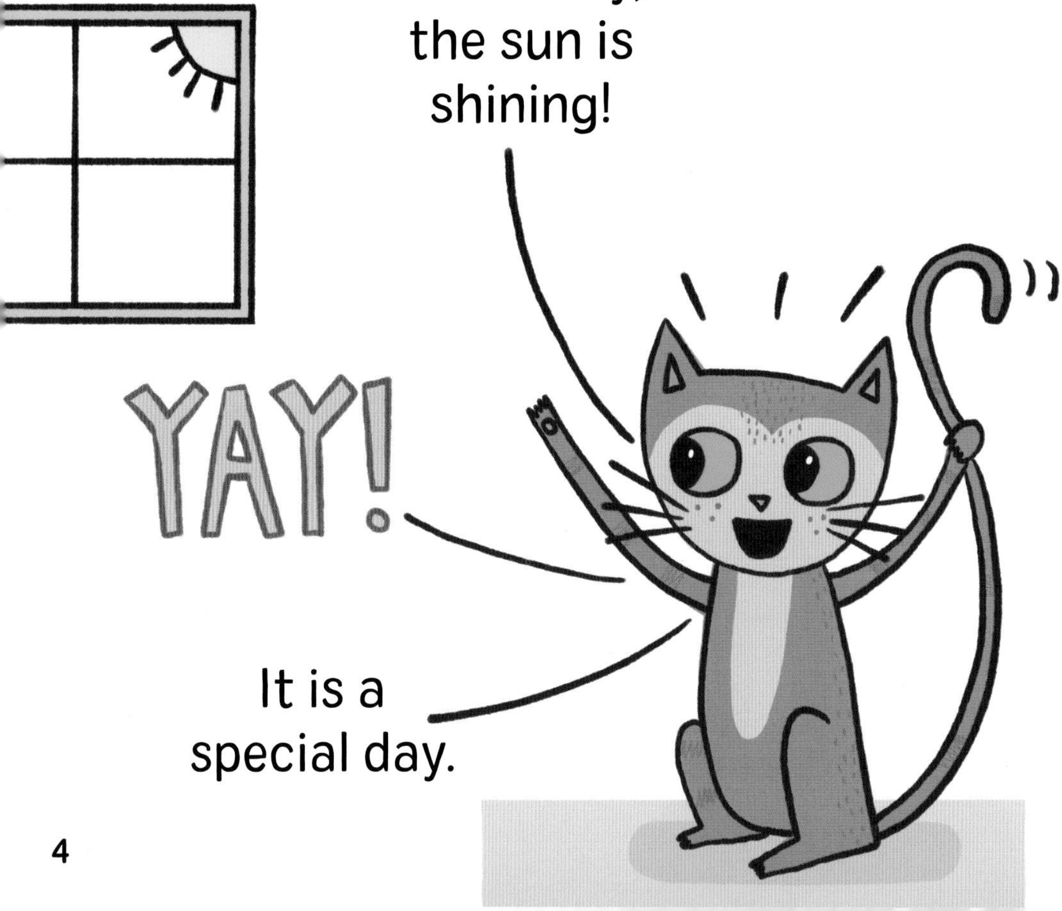
YAY!

It is a
special day.

Special things can be big.

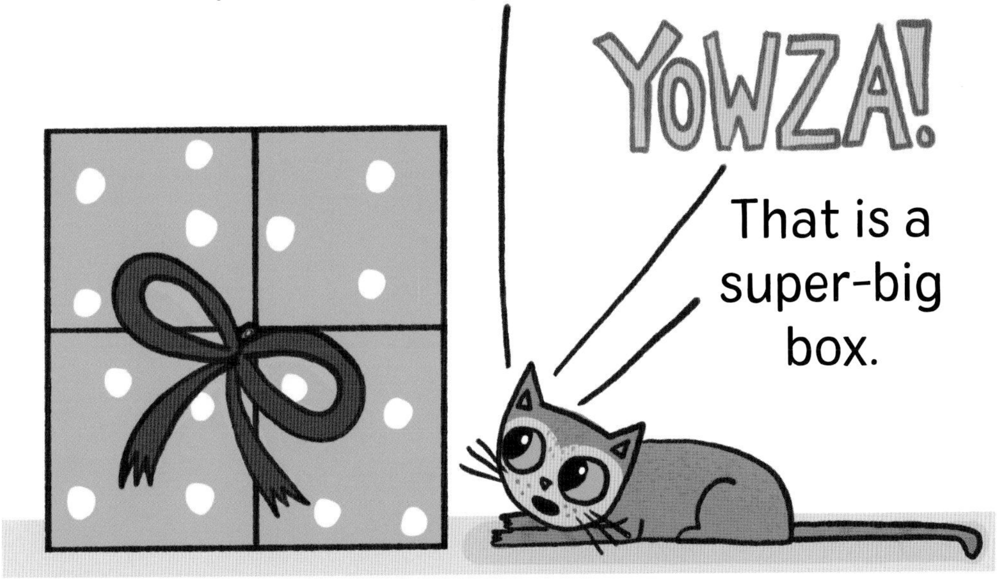
YOWZA!
That is a super-big box.

Special things can be small.

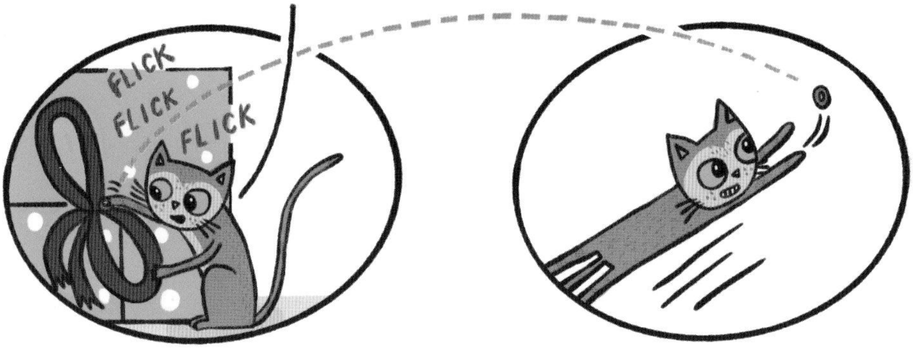
FLICK
FLICK
FLICK

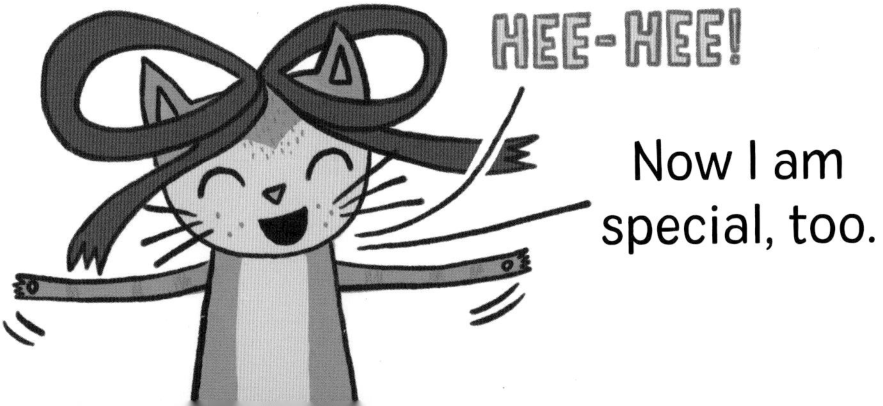
HEE-HEE!
Now I am special, too.

A special thing does not need a bow.

A special thing can be many things.

An old toy.

A favorite spot.

A yummy smell.

A surprise treat.

NUM NUM NUM

Step 1

Step 2

Or a fun sound.

FOOD
CRICK!
CRICK!

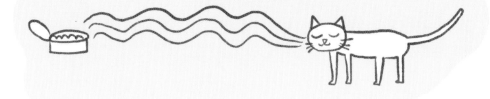

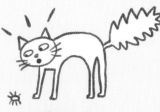

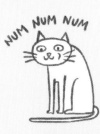

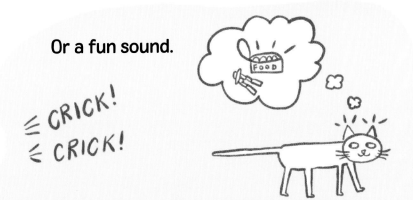

Today, I will celebrate
ALL the special things.

My insides will
be full of joy.

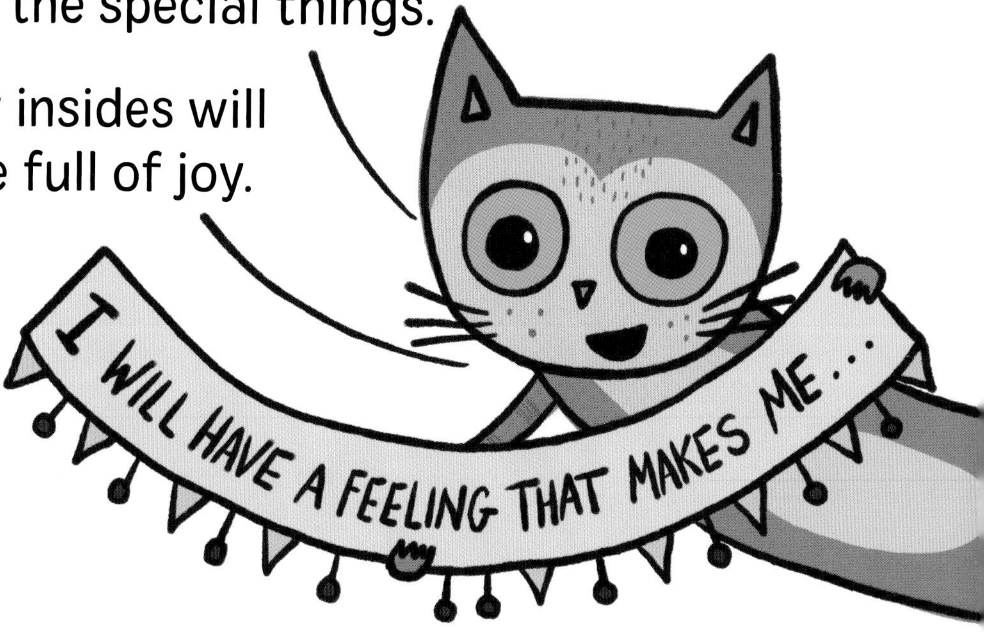
I WILL HAVE A FEELING THAT MAKES ME...

close my eyes,

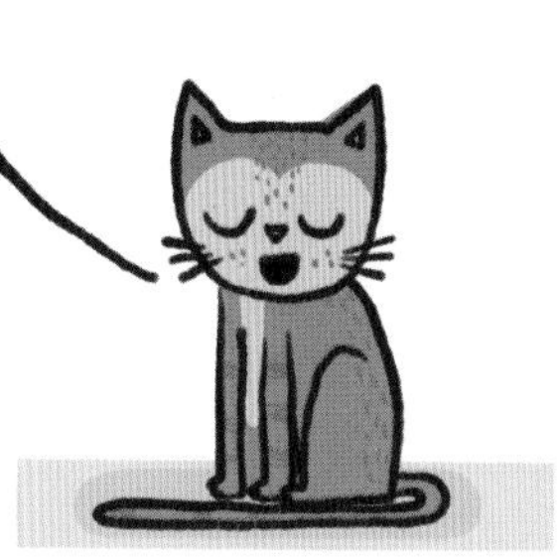

open my arms,

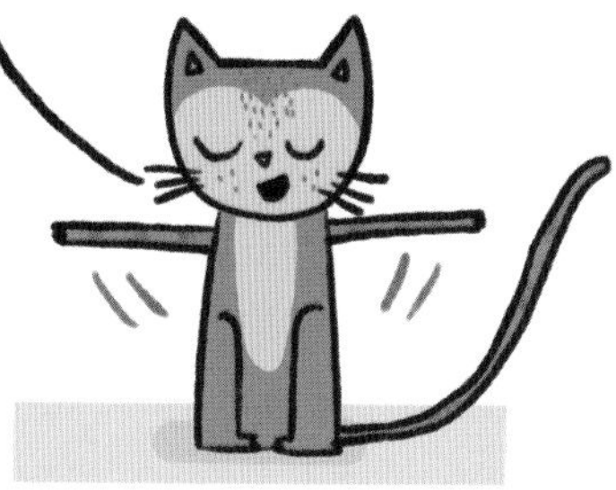

and spin in circles.

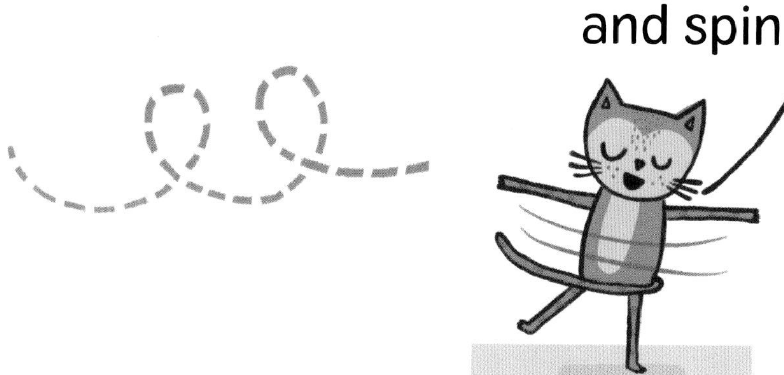

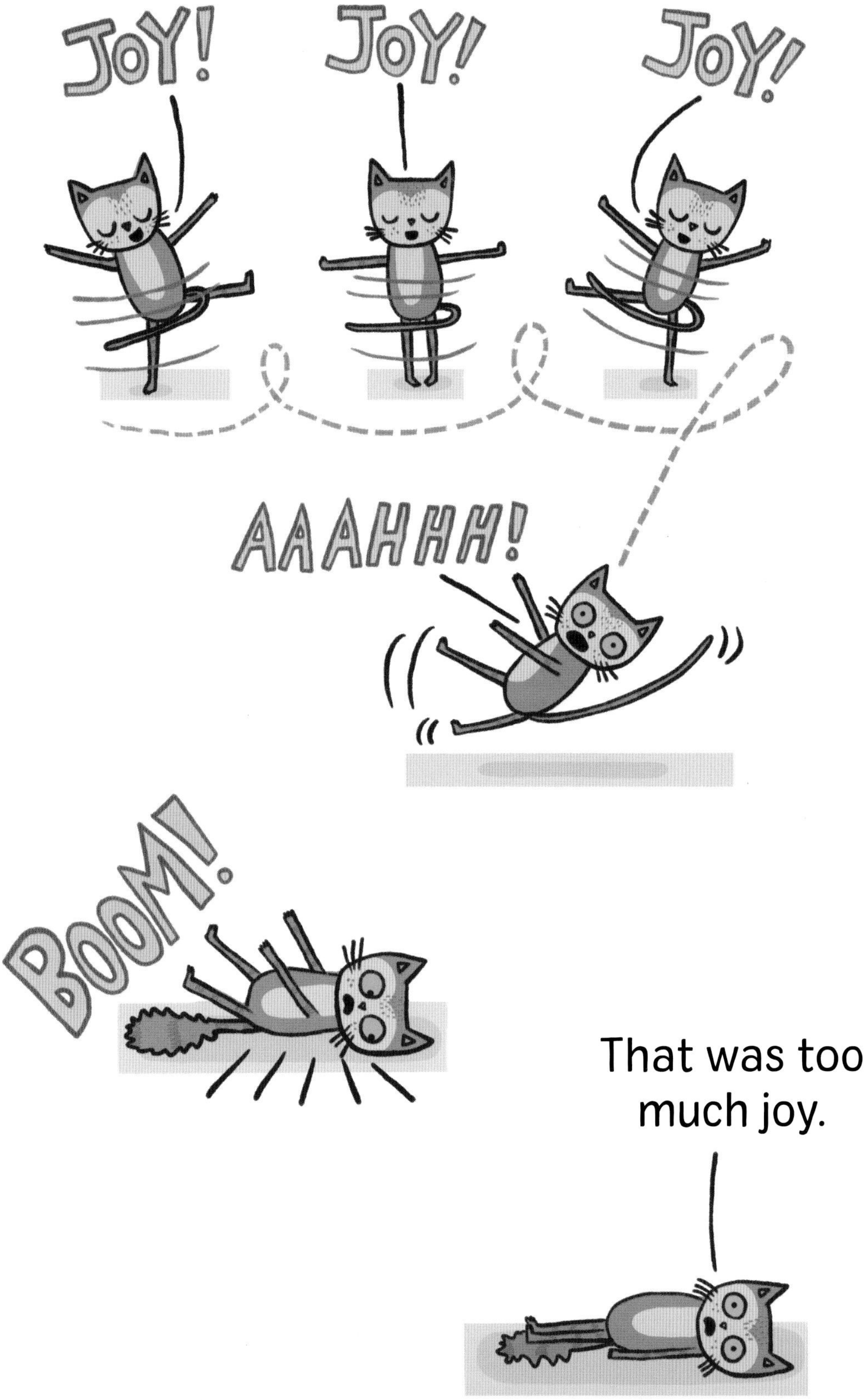
JOY!
JOY!
JOY!
AAAHHH!
BOOM!
That was too much joy.

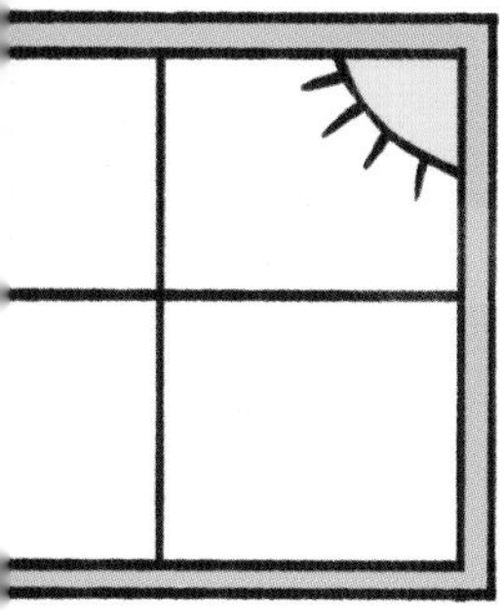

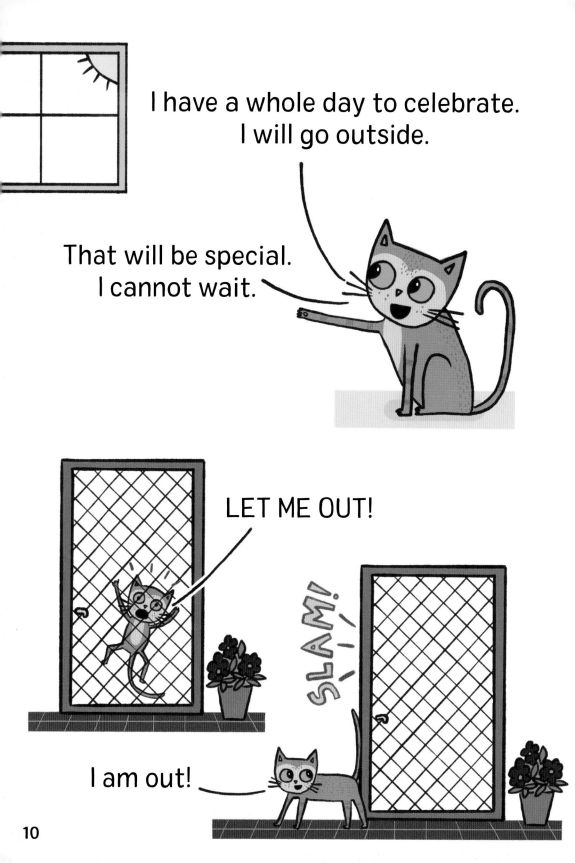

I have a whole day to celebrate.
I will go outside.

That will be special.
I cannot wait.

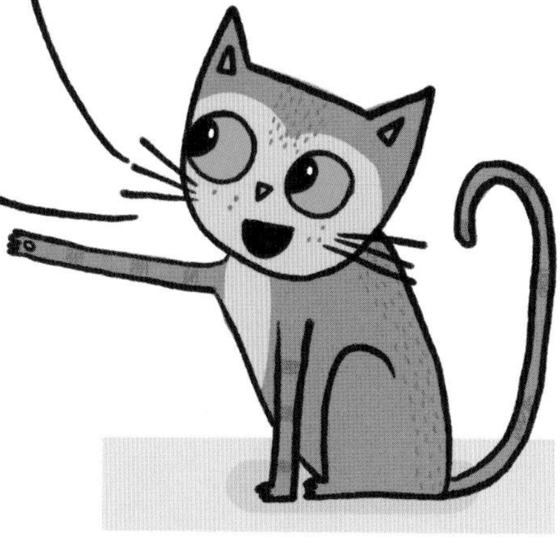

LET ME OUT!

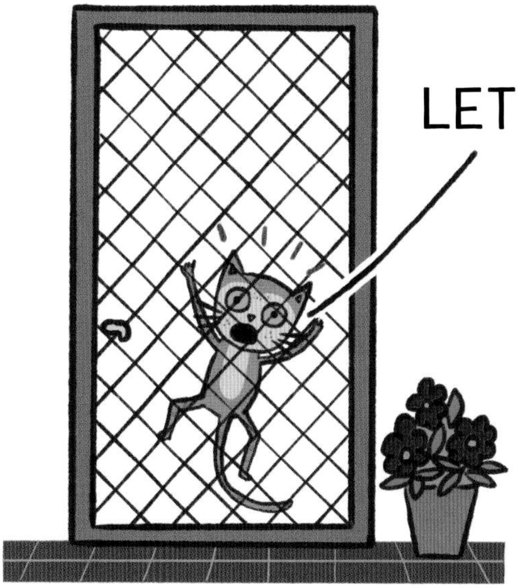

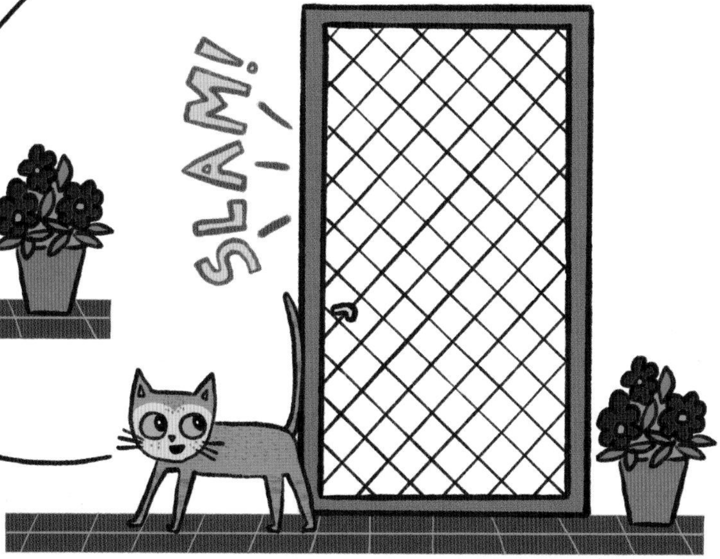
SLAM!

I am out!

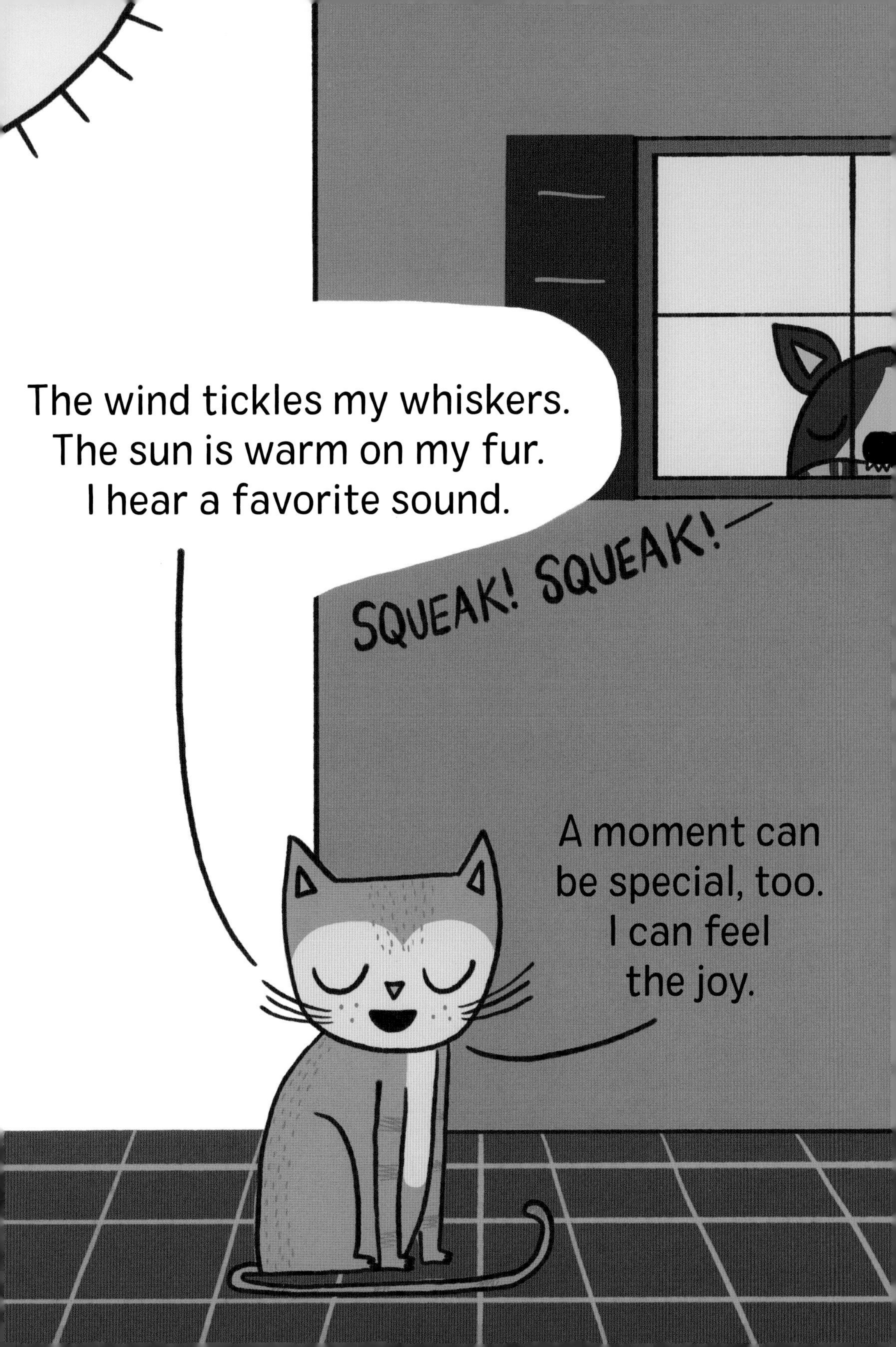
The wind tickles my whiskers.
The sun is warm on my fur.
I hear a favorite sound.
SQUEAK! SQUEAK!
A moment can be special, too. I can feel the joy.

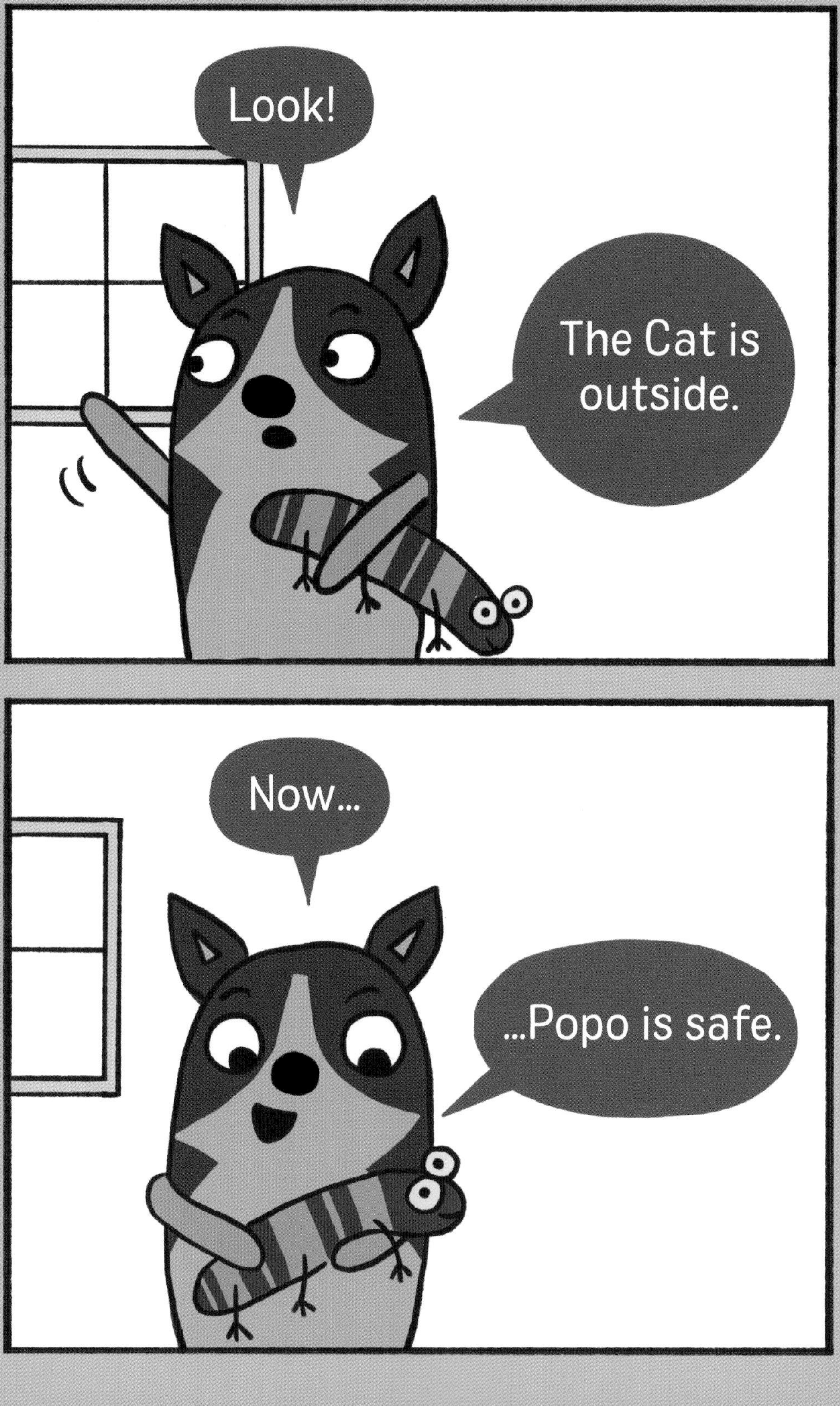
Look!
The Cat is outside.
Now...
...Popo is safe.

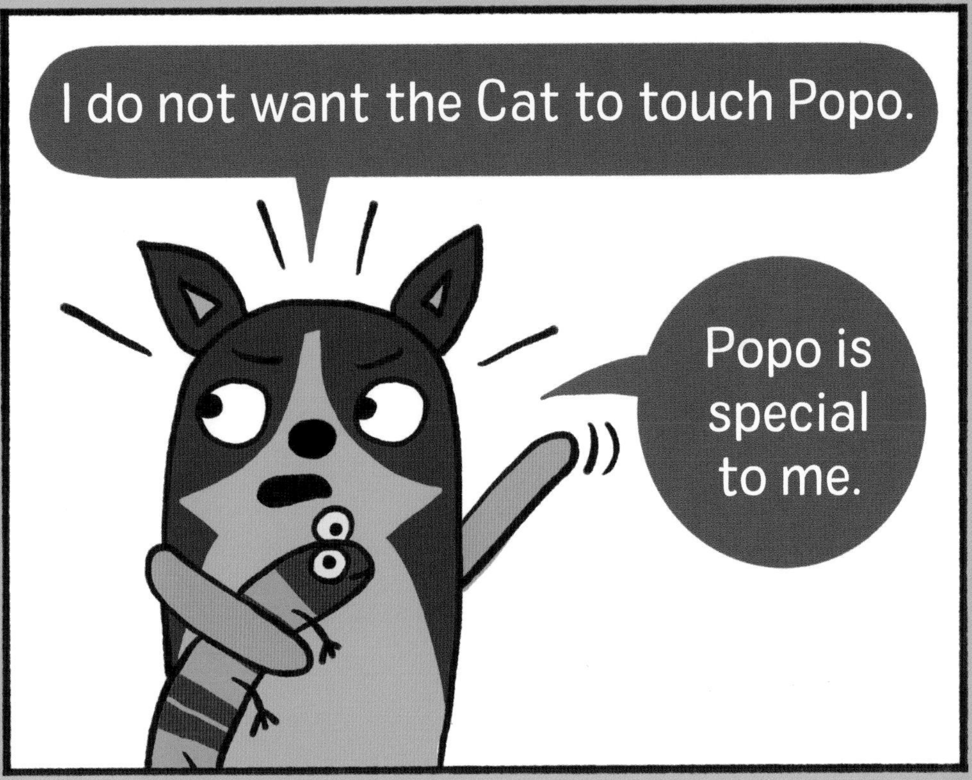
I do not want the Cat to touch Popo.
Popo is special to me.

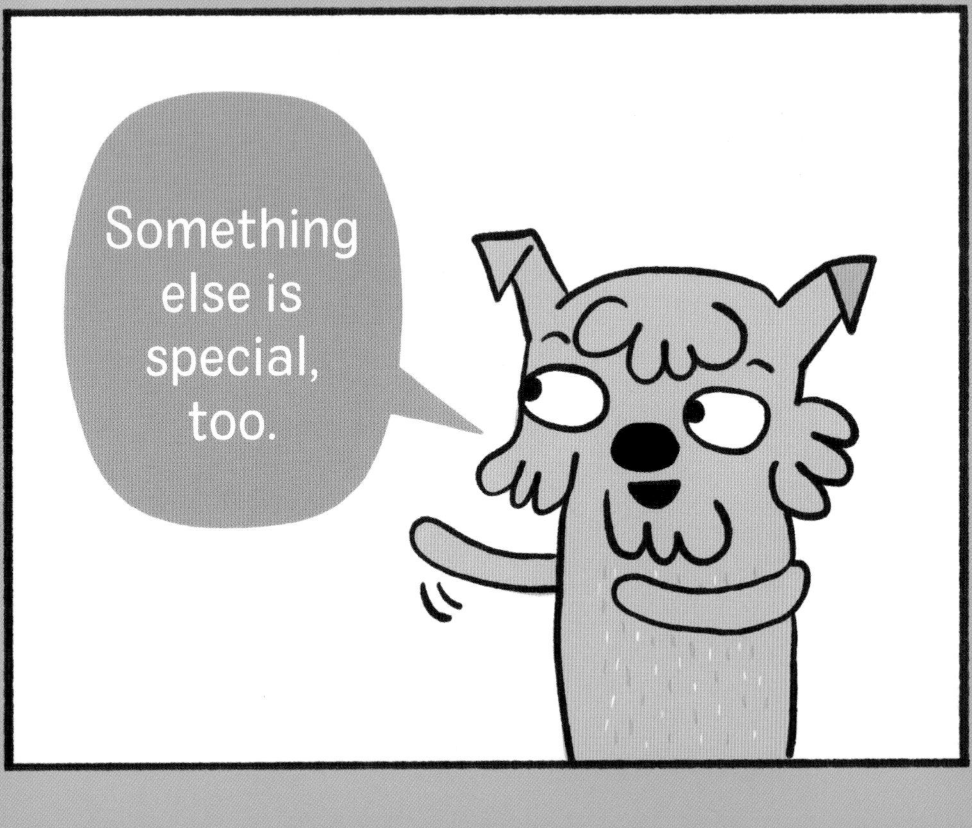
Something else is special, too.

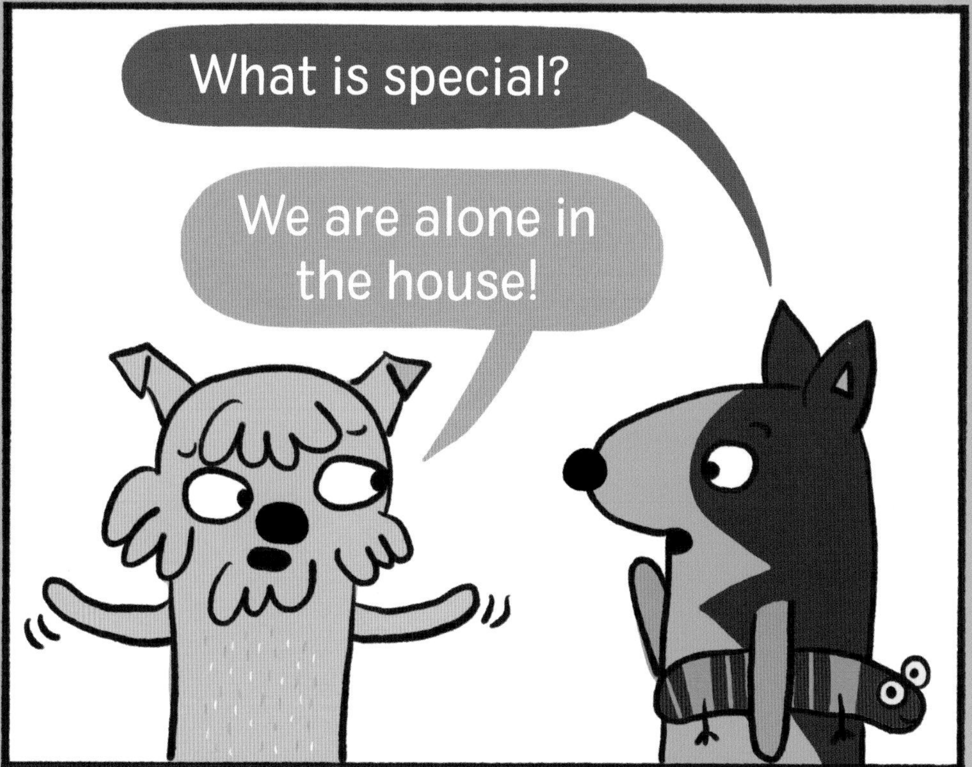
What is special?
We are alone in the house!

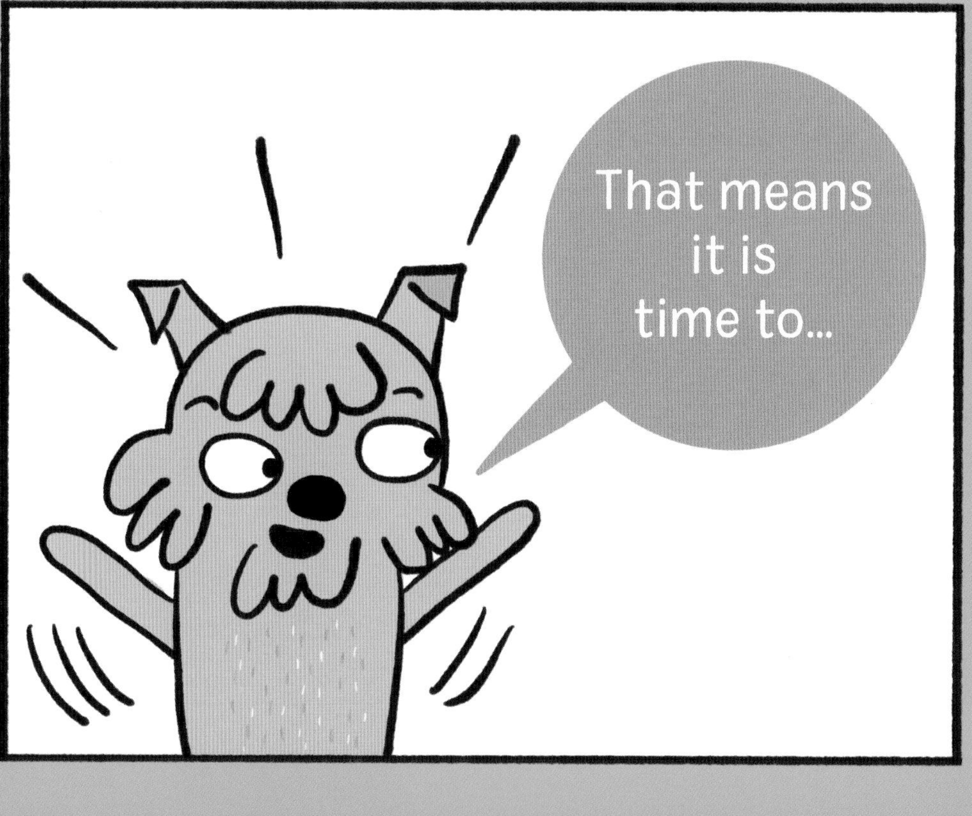
That means it is time to…

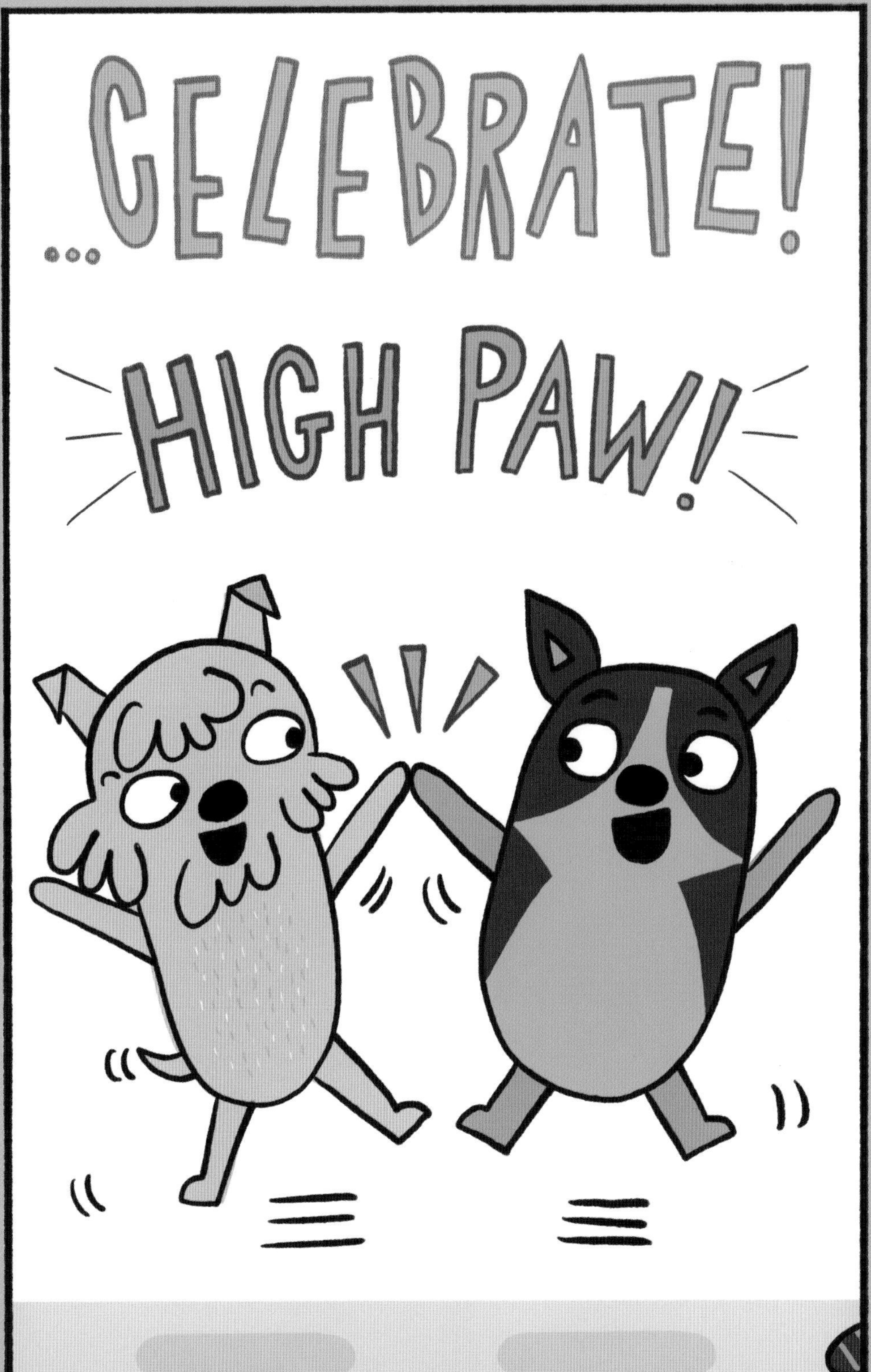
...CELEBRATE!
HIGH PAW!

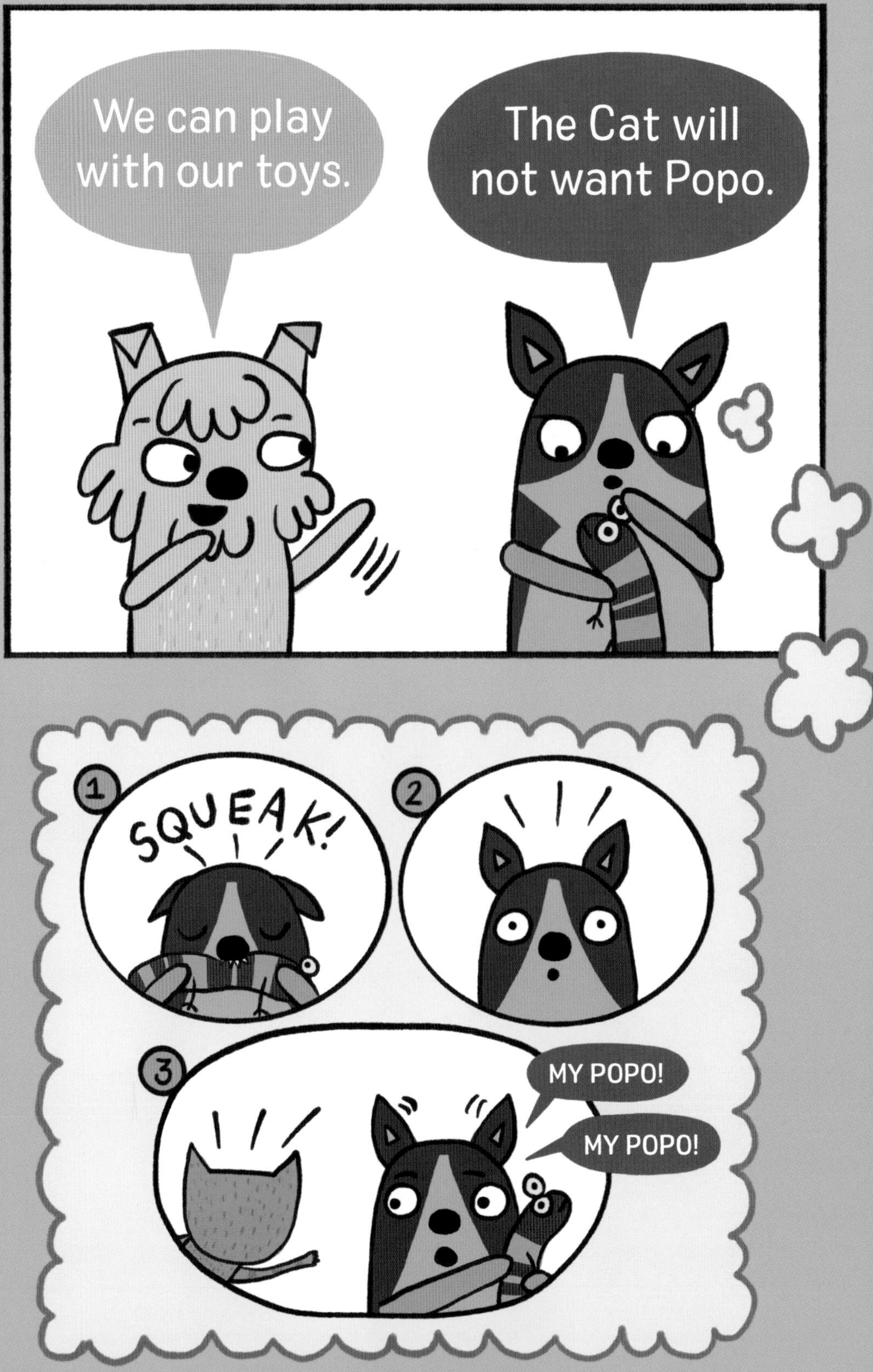
We can play with our toys.
The Cat will not want Popo.
SQUEAK!
MY POPO!
MY POPO!

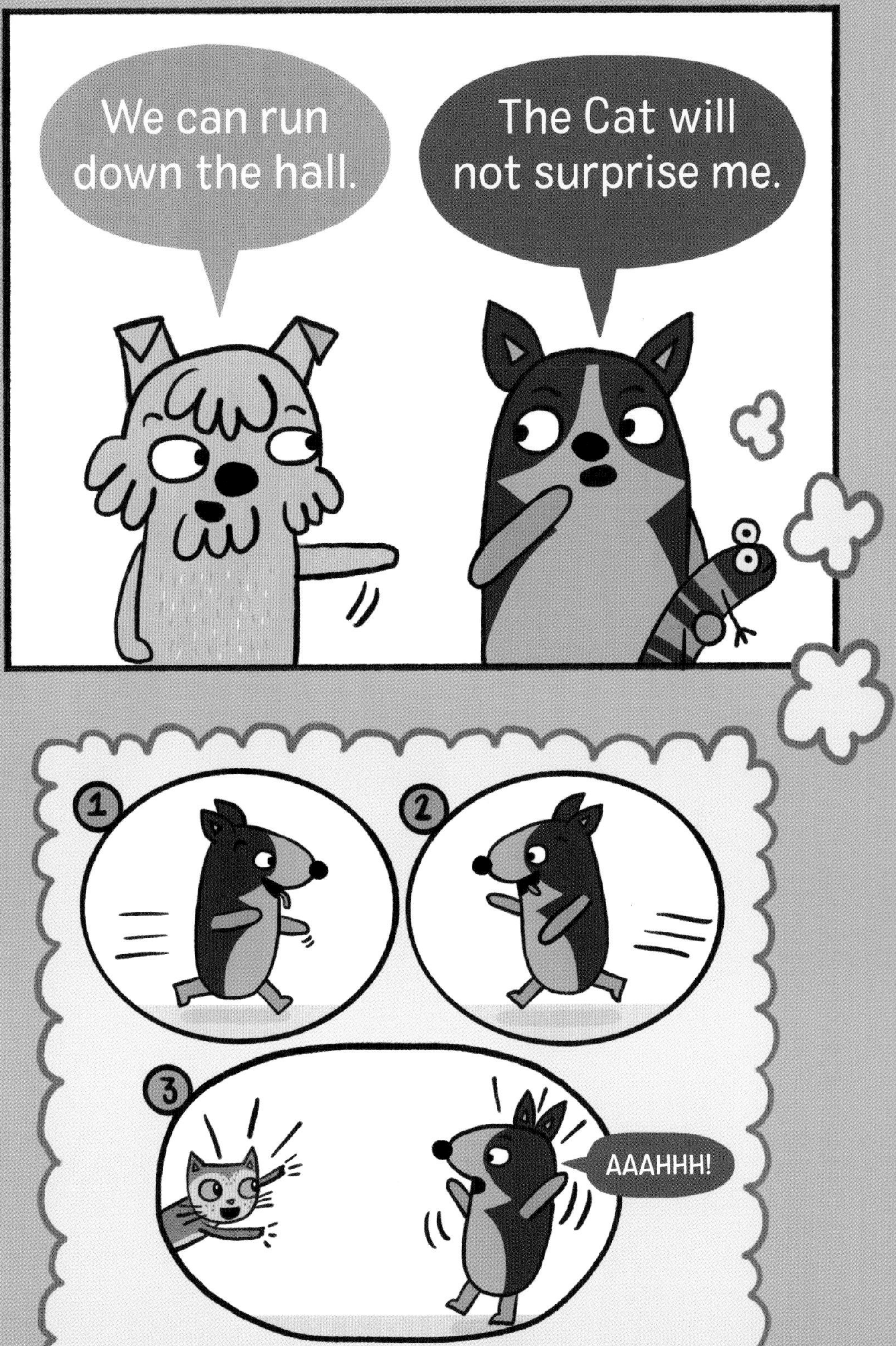
We can run down the hall.
The Cat will not surprise me.
1
2
3
AAAHHH!

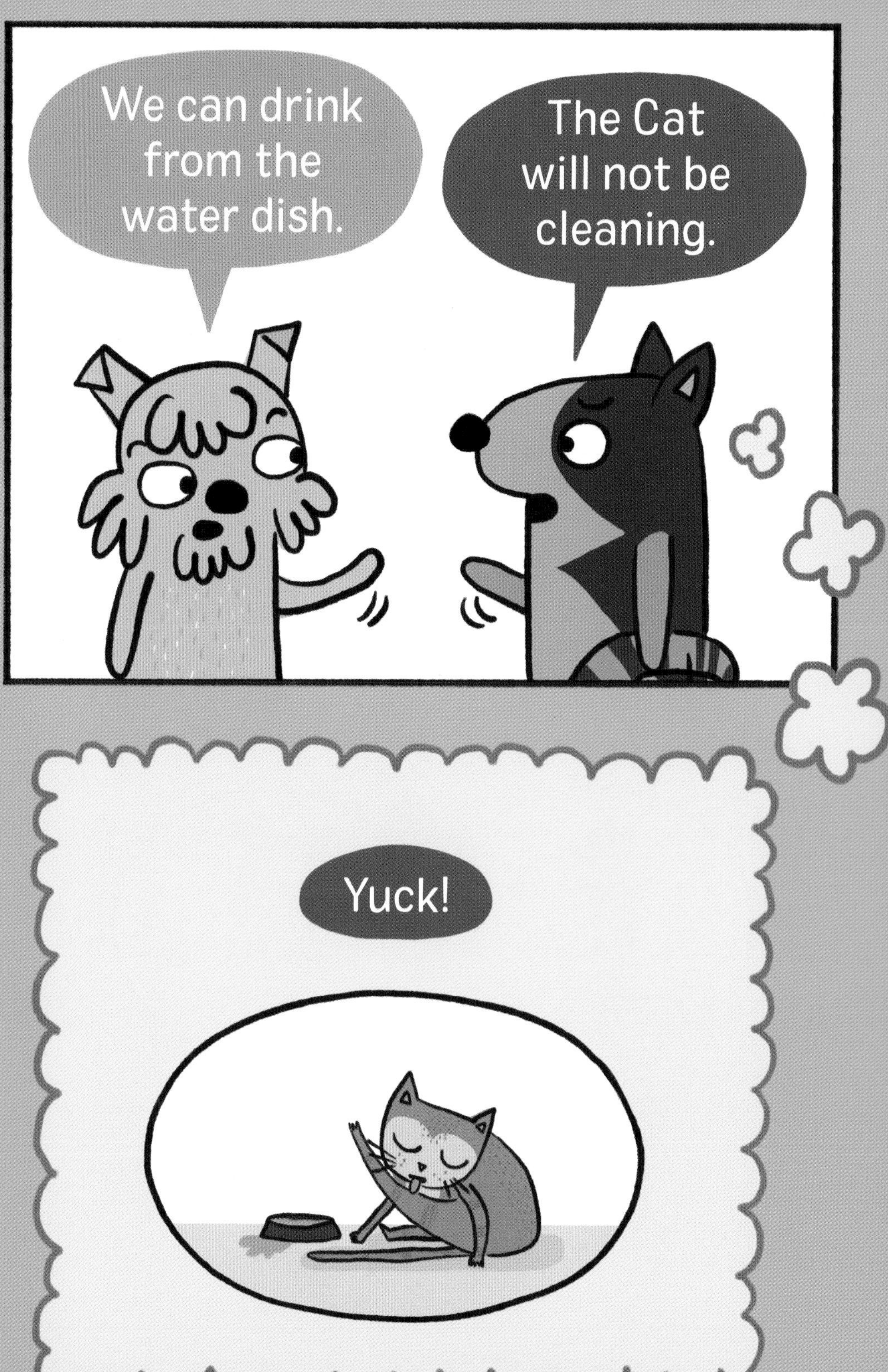
We can drink from the water dish.
The Cat will not be cleaning.
Yuck!

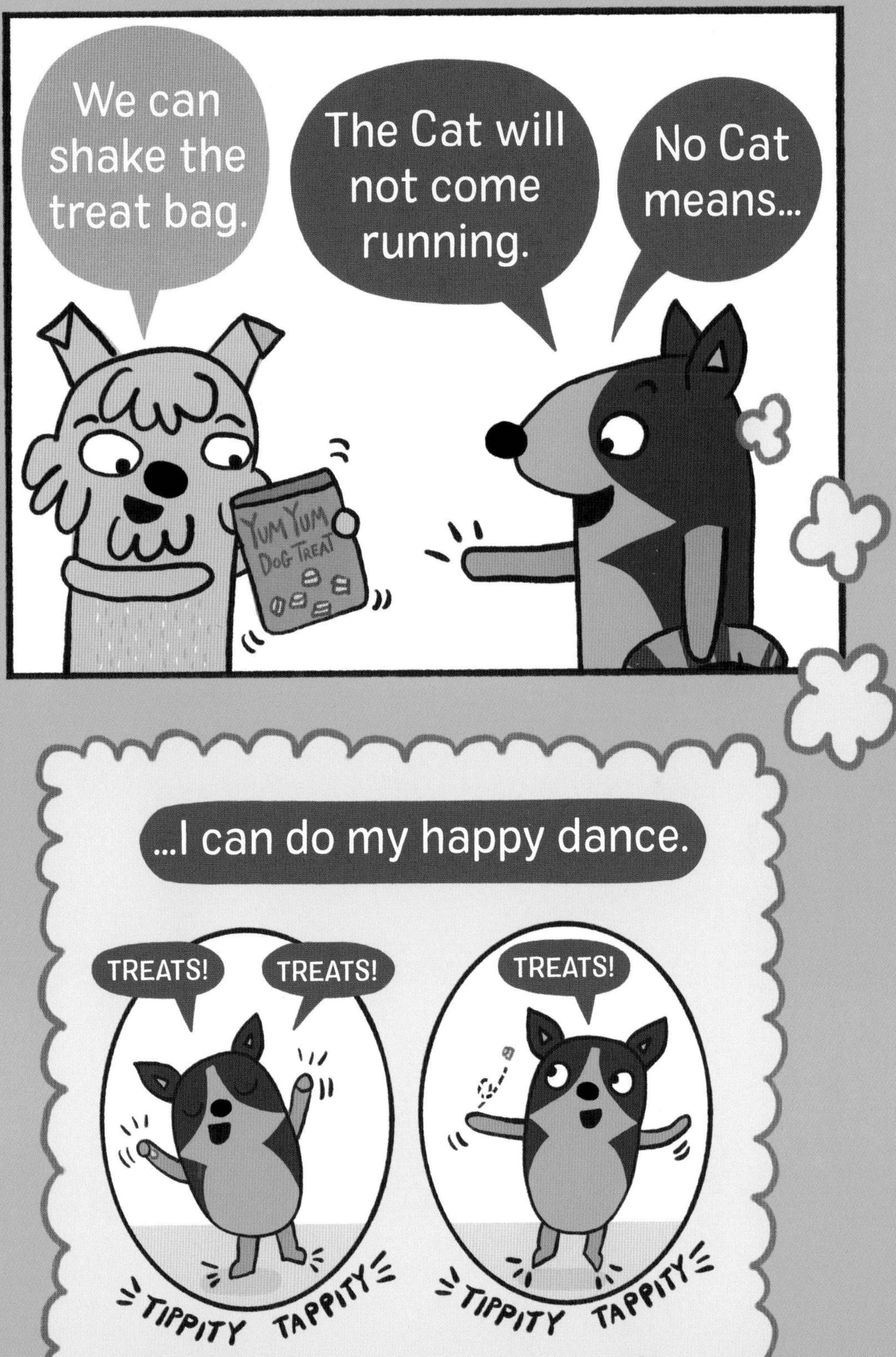
We can shake the treat bag.
The Cat will not come running.
No Cat means...
YUM YUM DOG TREAT
...I can do my happy dance.
TREATS!
TREATS!
TIPPITY TAPPITY
TREATS!
TIPPITY TAPPITY

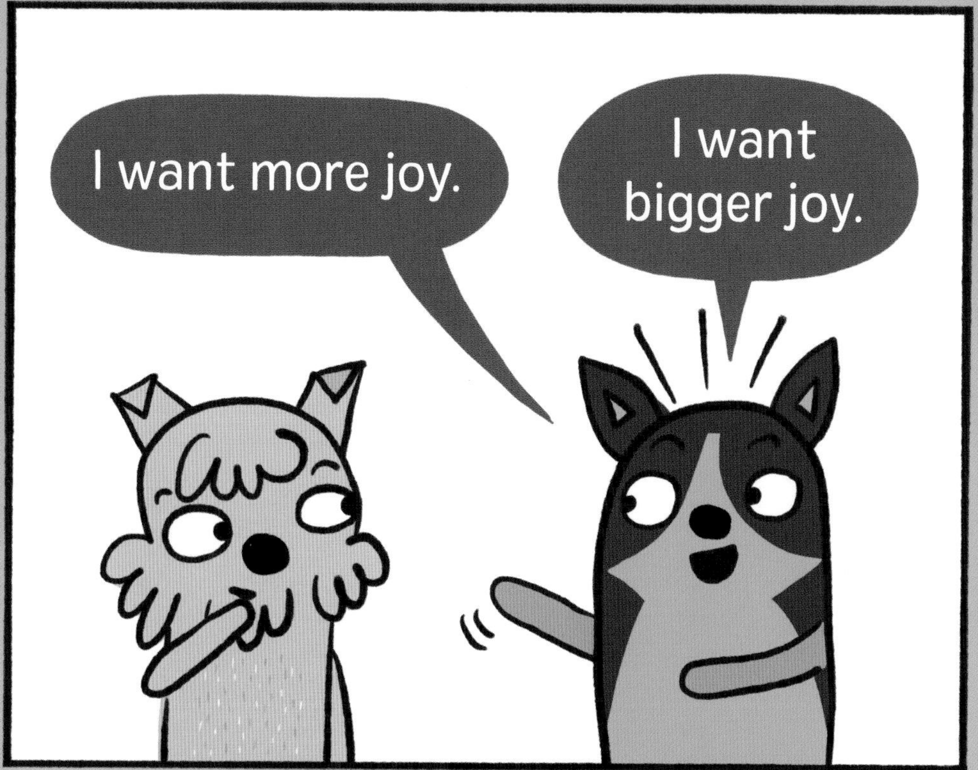
I want more joy.
I want bigger joy.

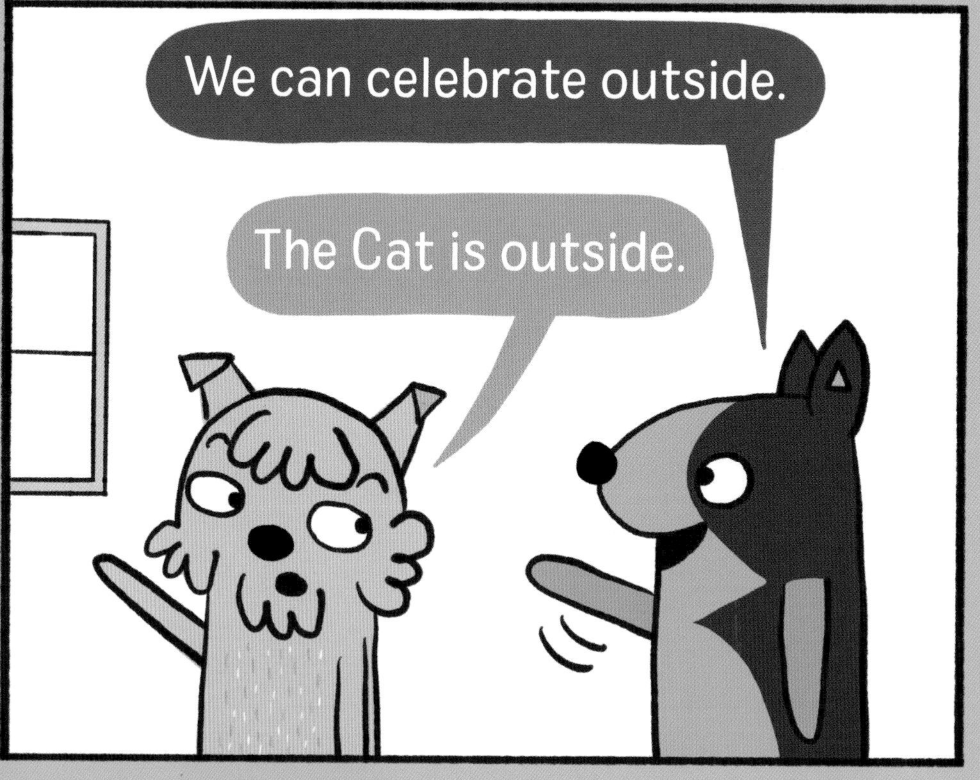
We can celebrate outside.
The Cat is outside.

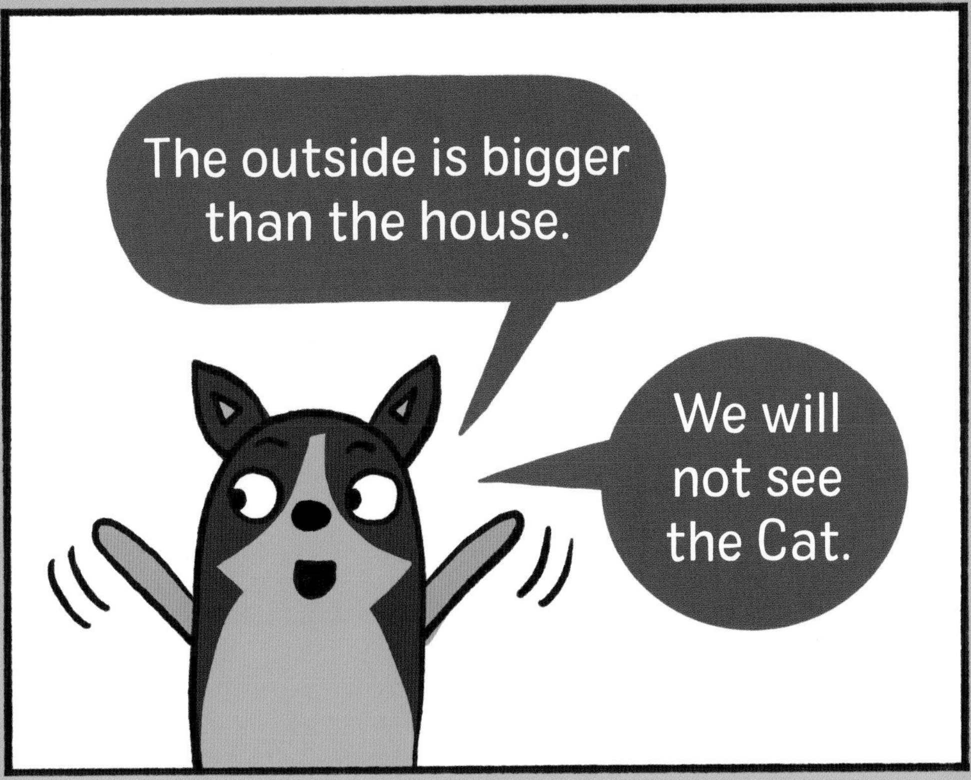
The outside is bigger than the house.
We will not see the Cat.

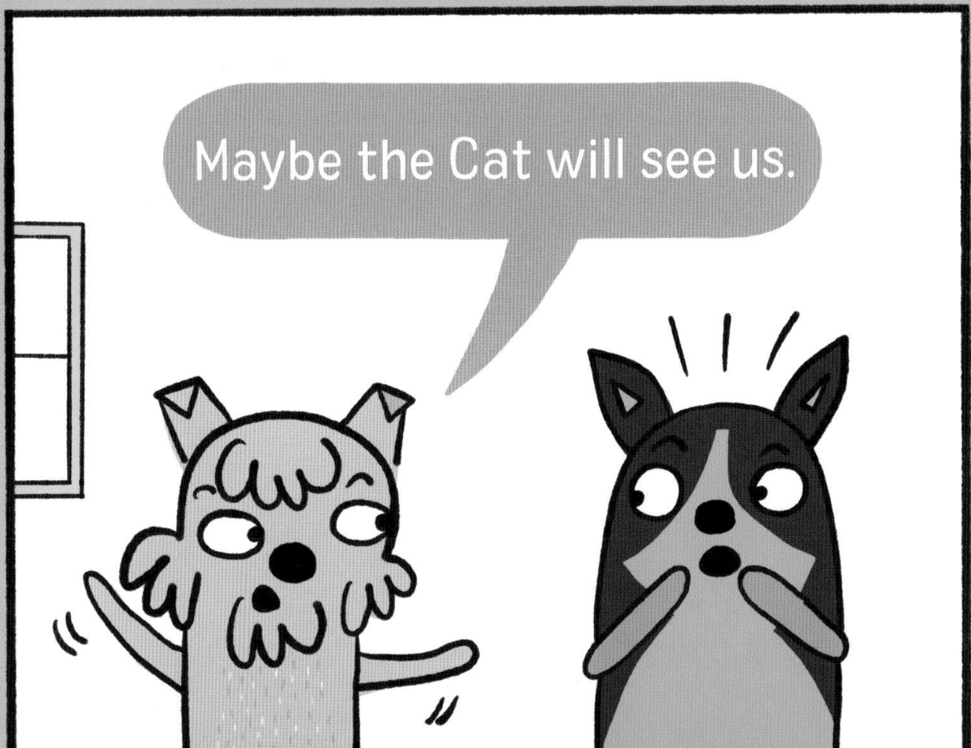
Maybe the Cat will see us.

And now I will celebrate...

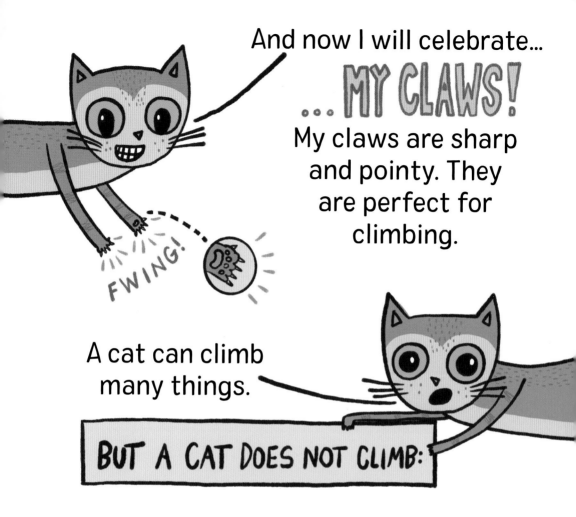

...MY CLAWS!

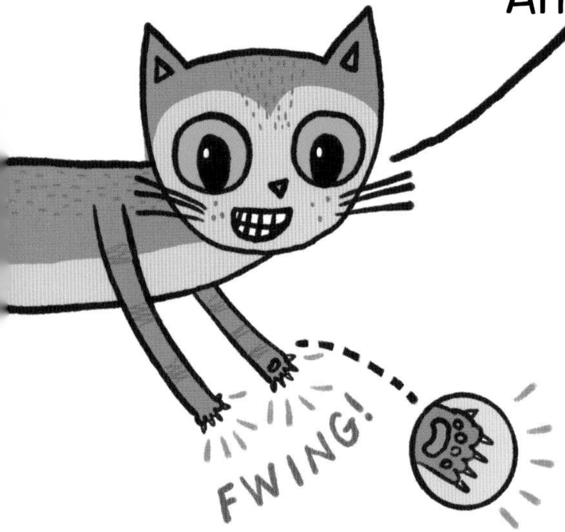
FWING!

My claws are sharp and pointy. They are perfect for climbing.

A cat can climb many things.

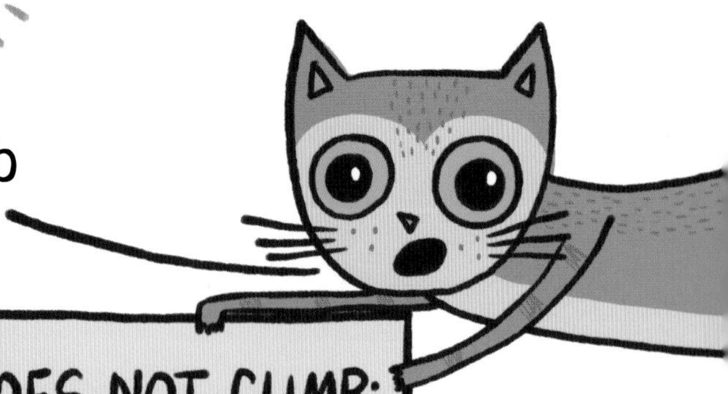

BUT A CAT DOES NOT CLIMB:

flagpoles—too slippery,

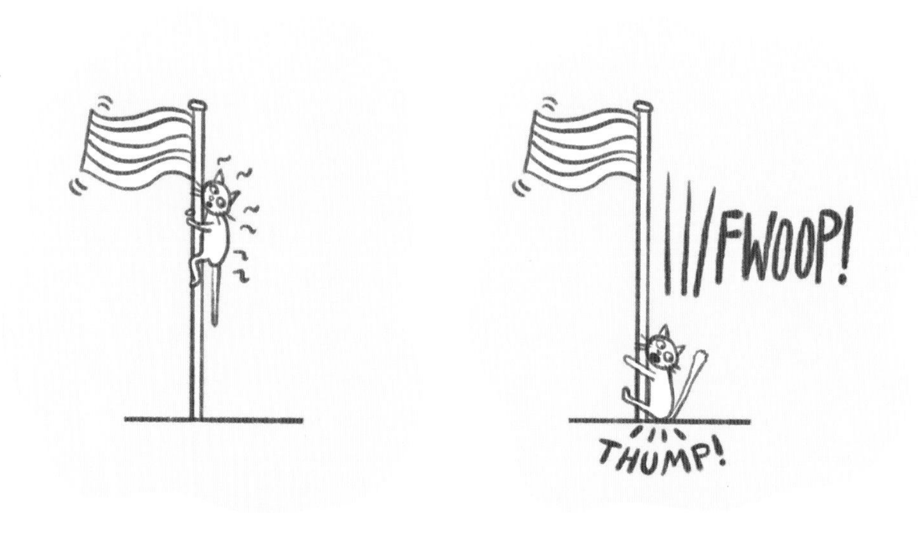
FWOOP!
THUMP!

telephone poles—too zappy,

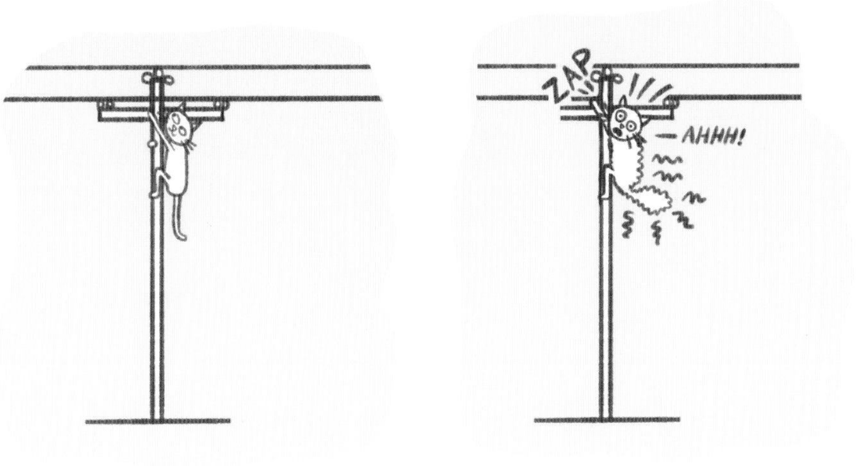
ZAP
AHHH!

and ropes—too grabby.

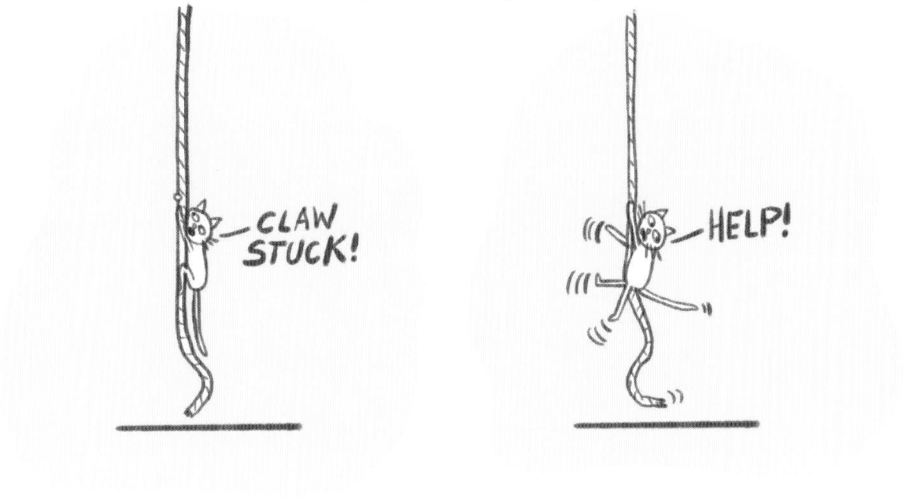
CLAW STUCK!
HELP!

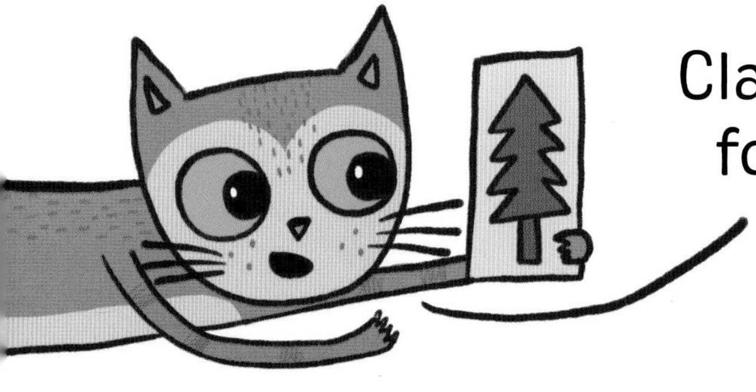

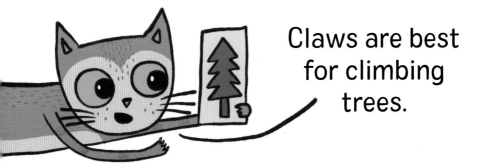

Claws are best for climbing trees.

CLAWS OUT!

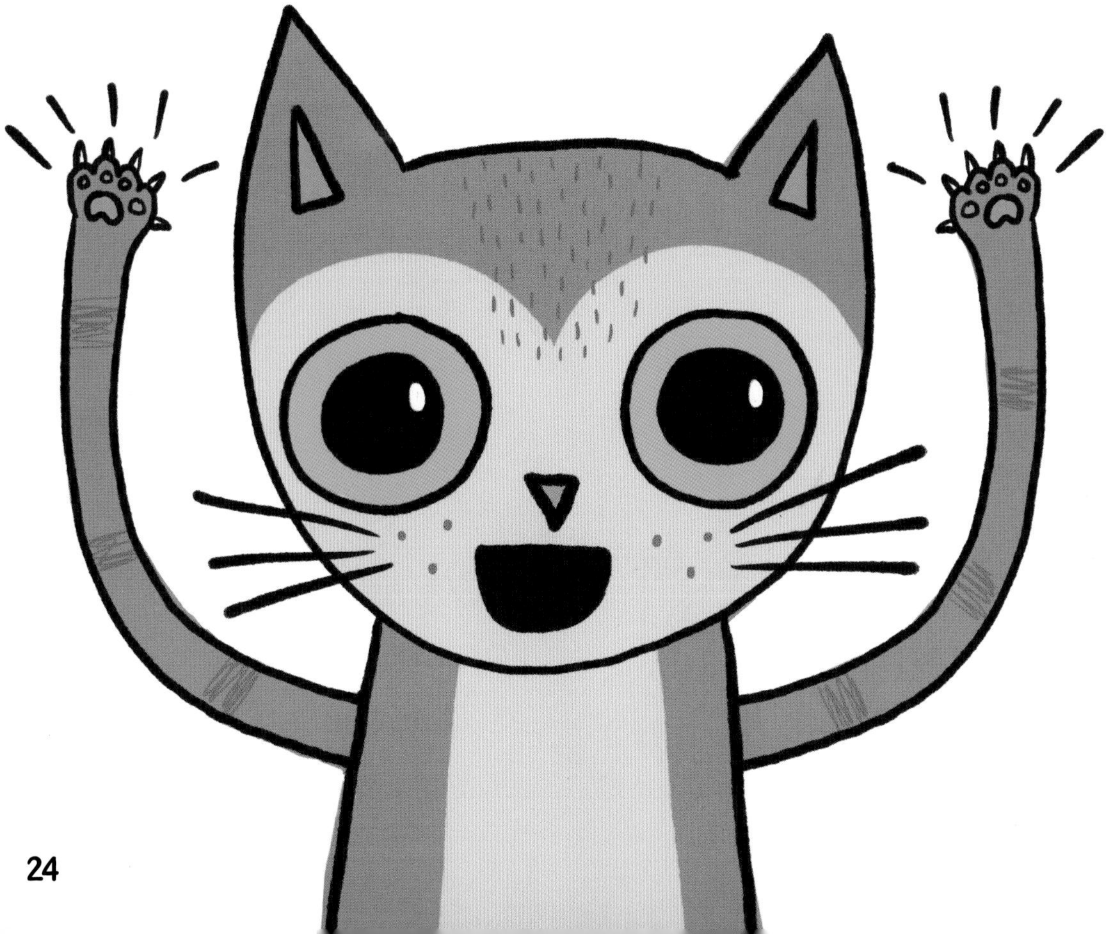

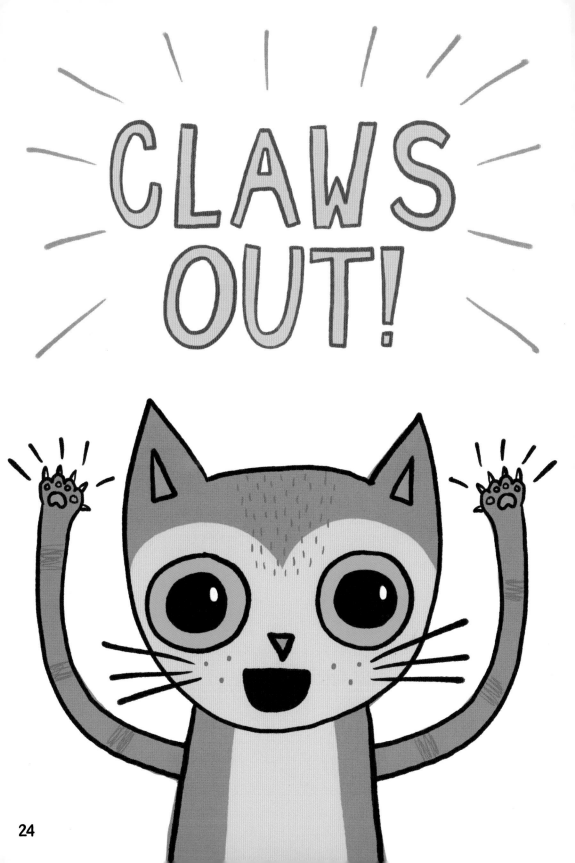

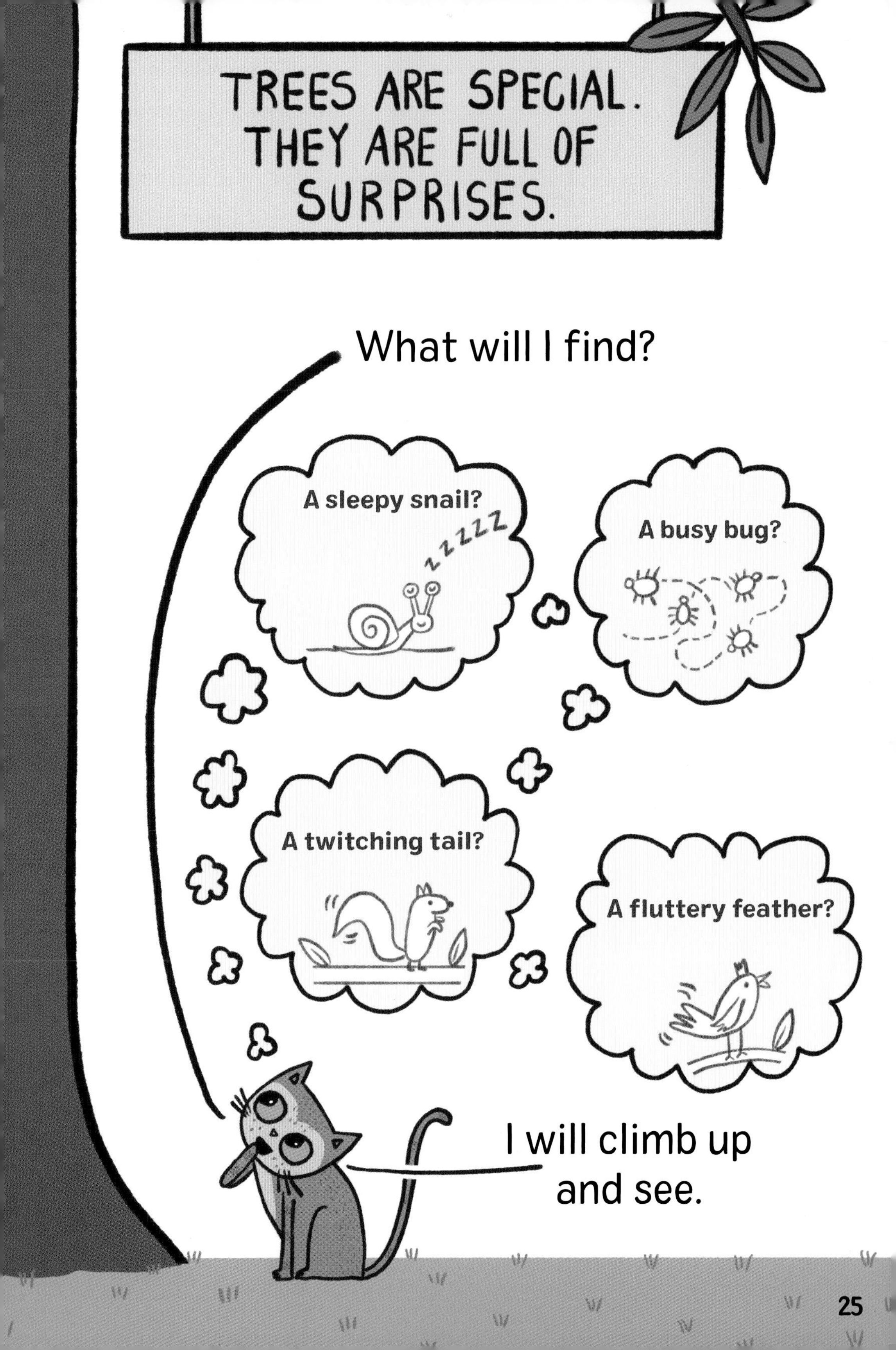
TREES ARE SPECIAL. THEY ARE FULL OF SURPRISES.
What will I find?
A sleepy snail?
ZZZZZ
A busy bug?
A twitching tail?
A fluttery feather?
I will climb up and see.

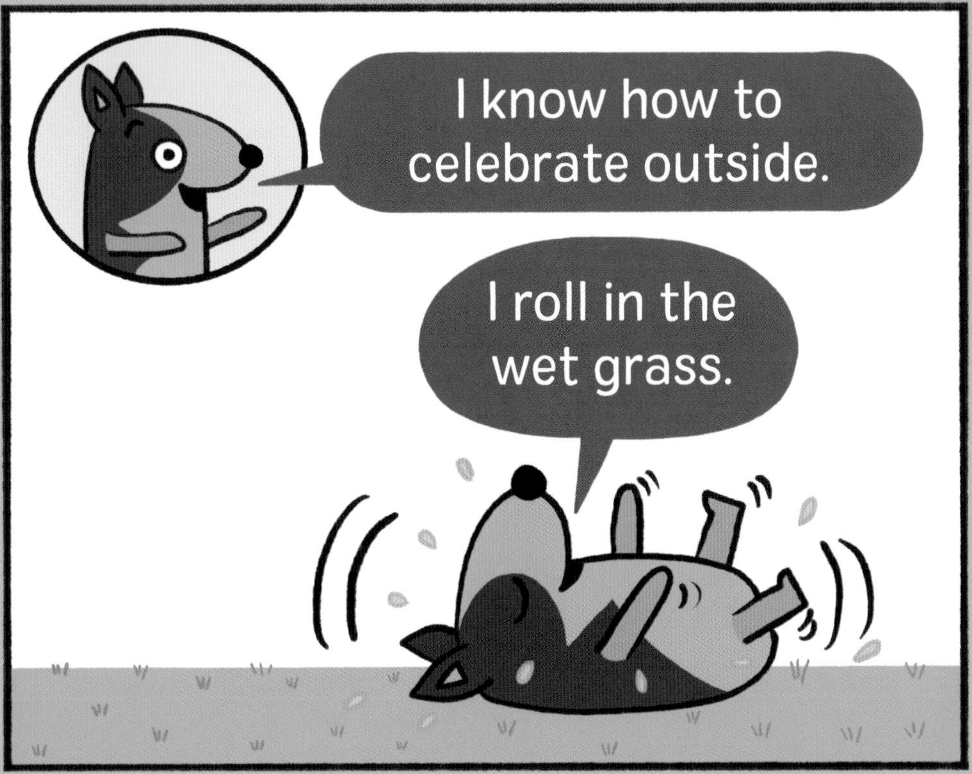
I know how to celebrate outside.
I roll in the wet grass.

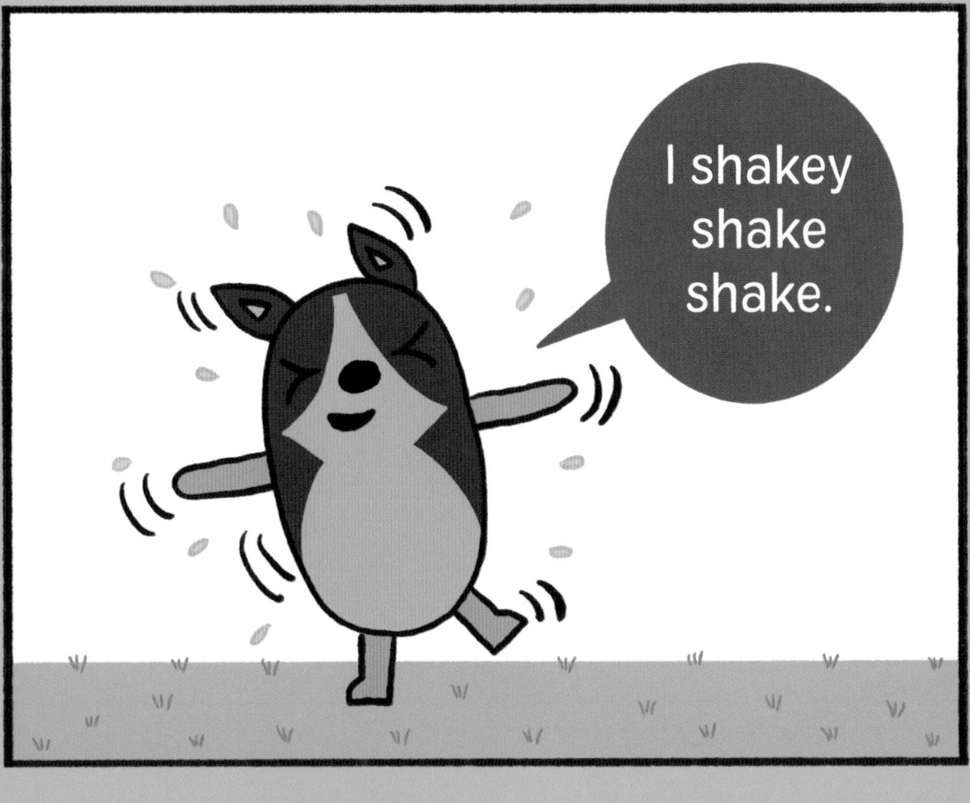
I shakey shake shake.

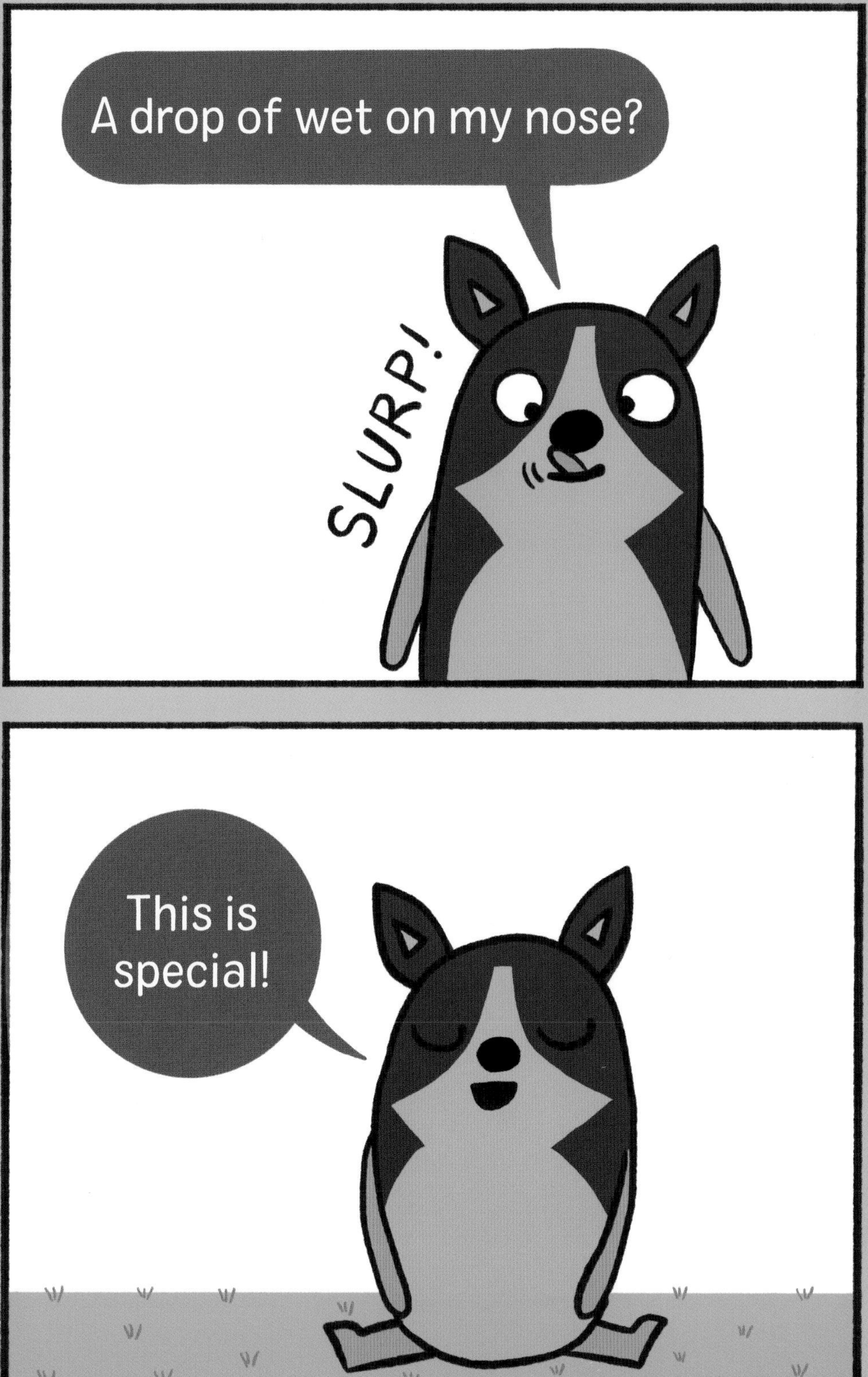
A drop of wet on my nose?
SLURP!
This is special!

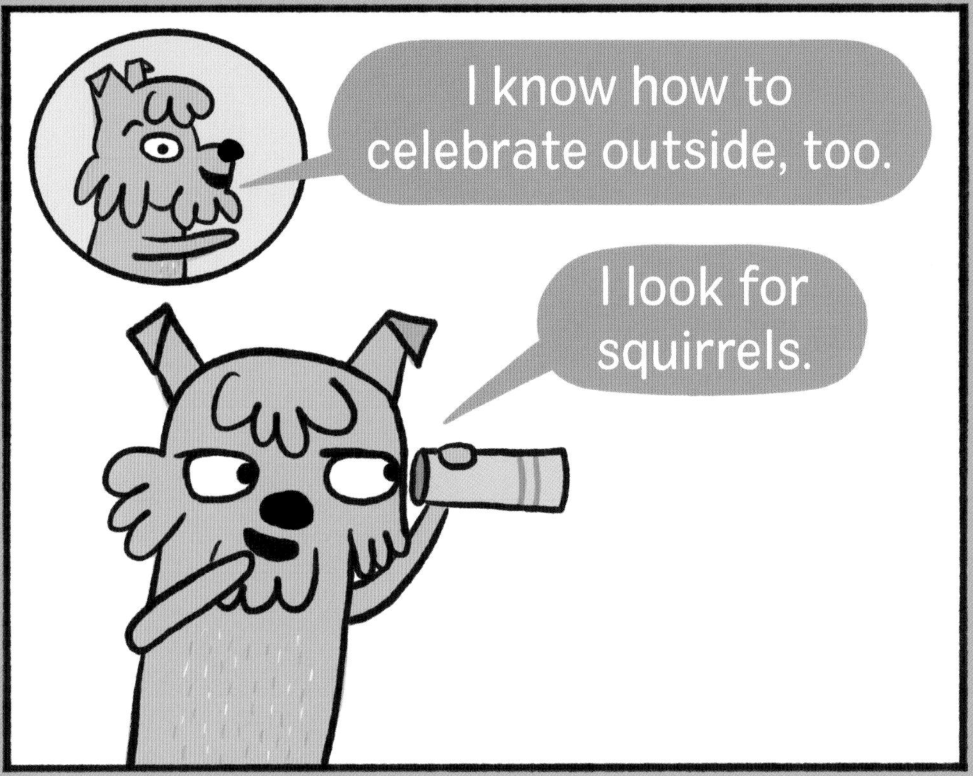
I know how to celebrate outside, too.
I look for squirrels.

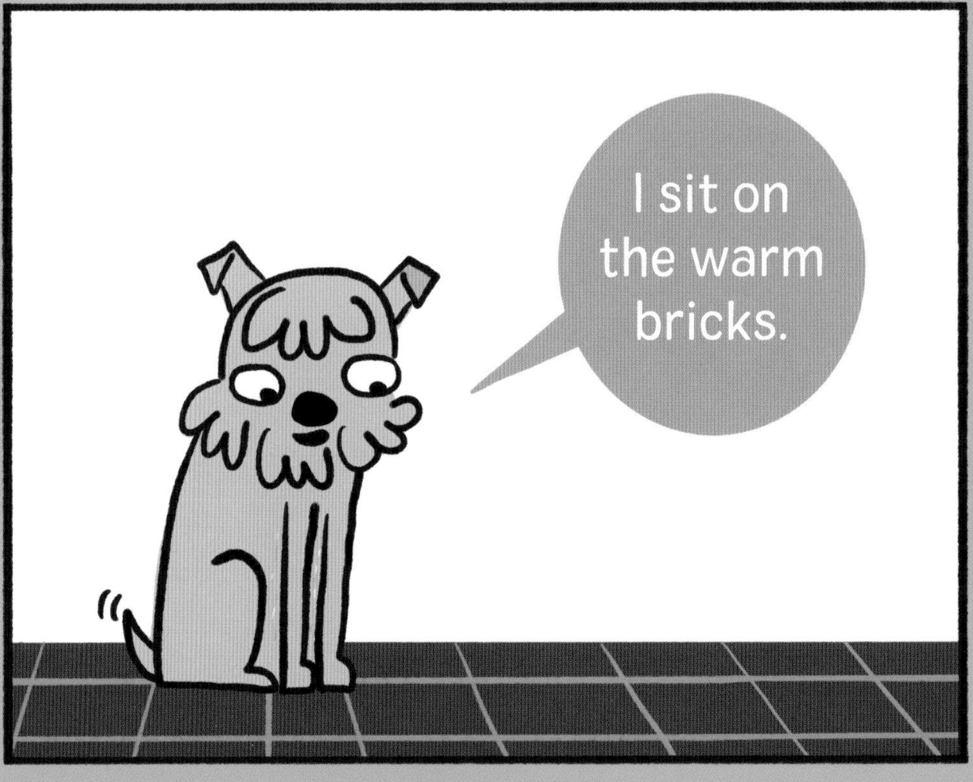
I sit on the warm bricks.

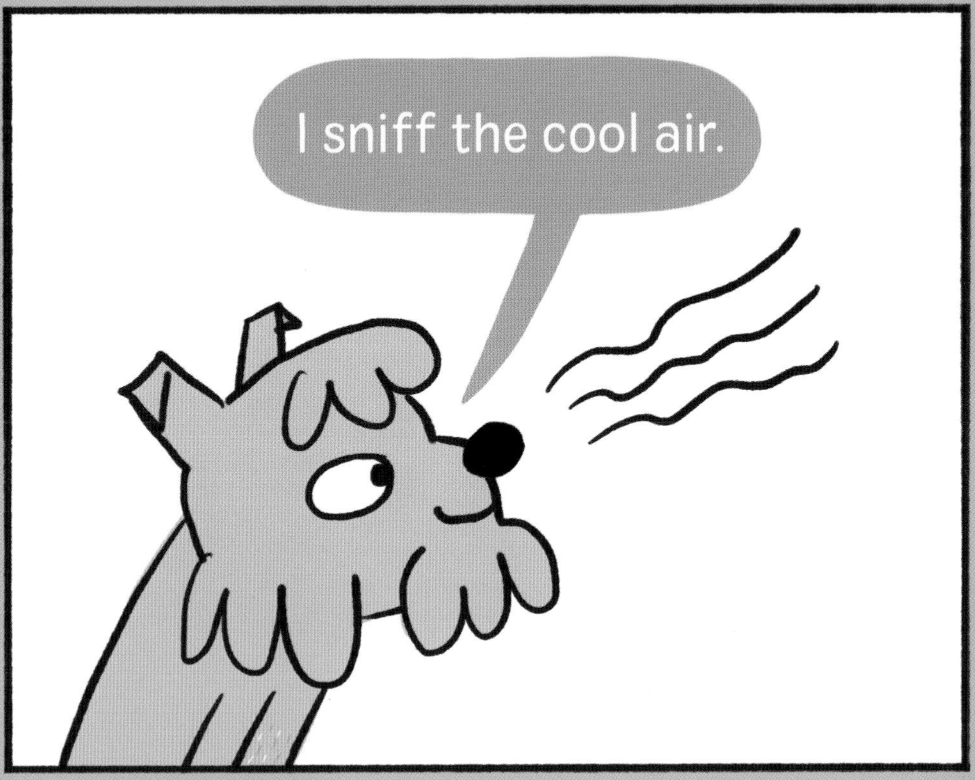
I sniff the cool air.

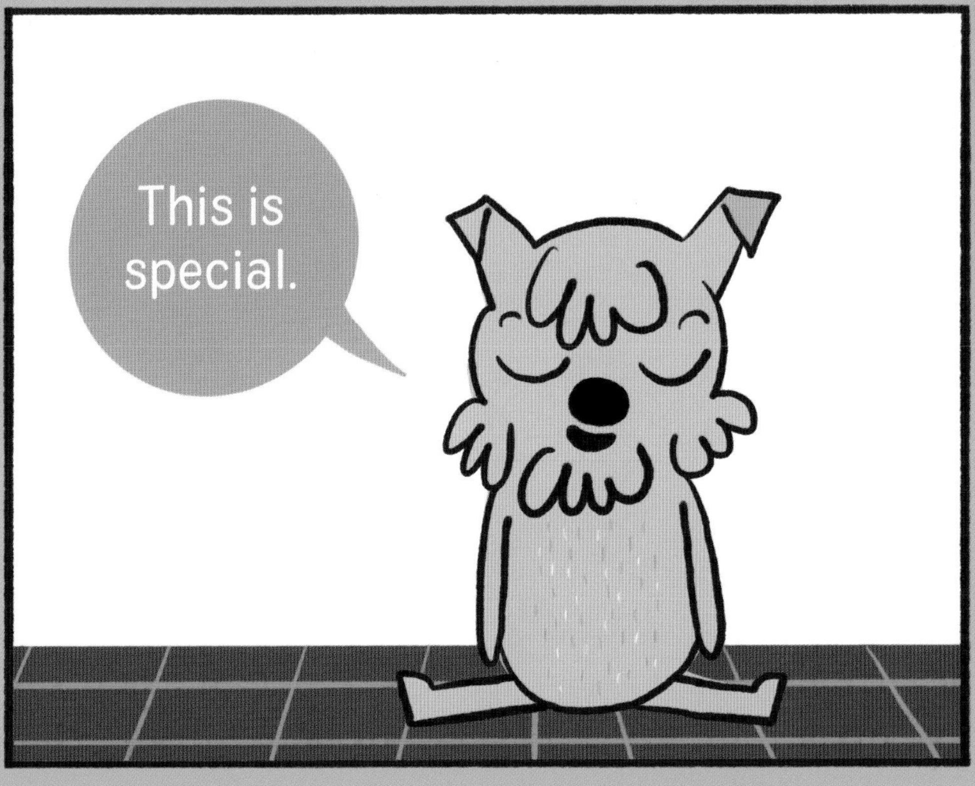
This is special.

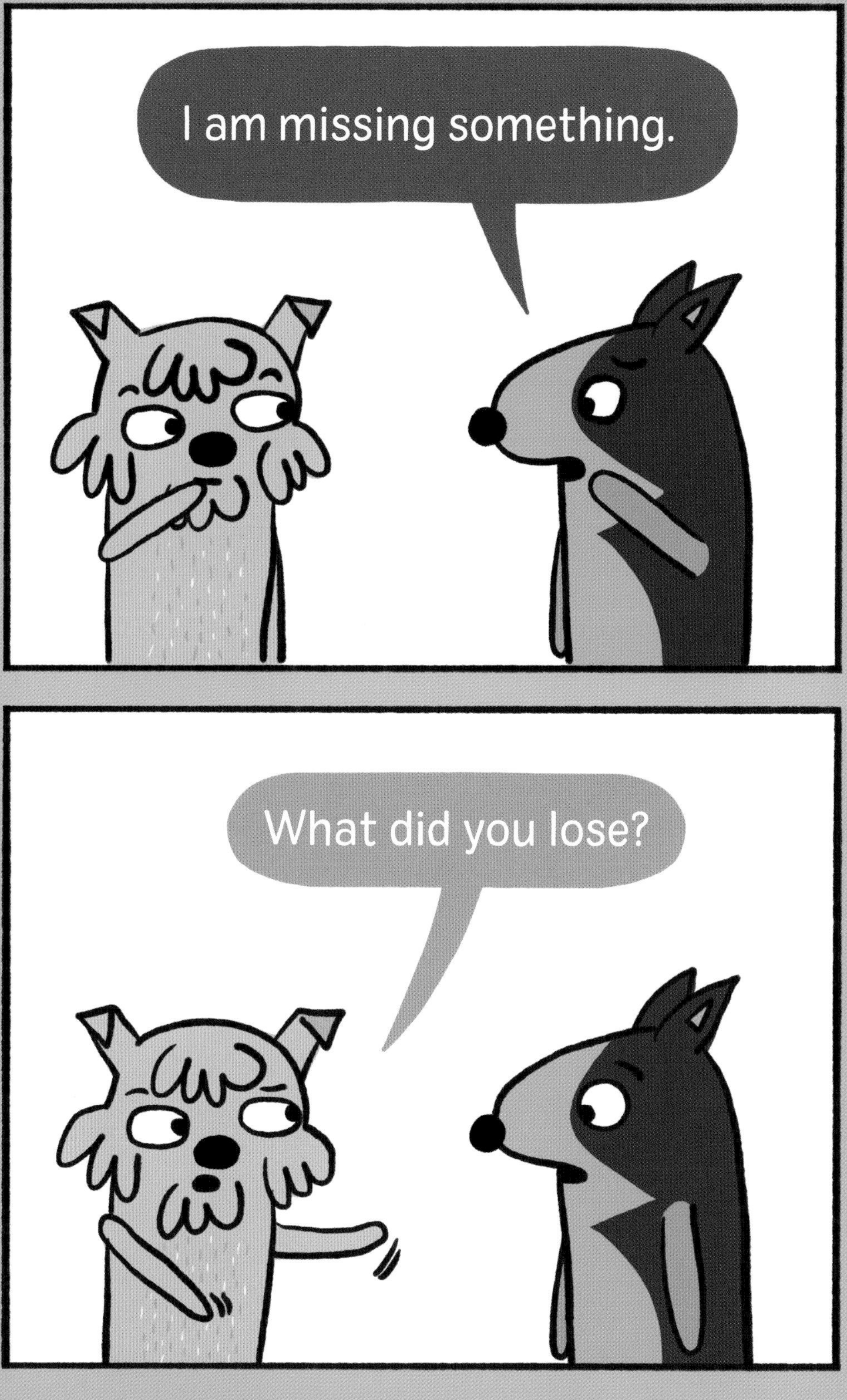
I am missing something.
What did you lose?

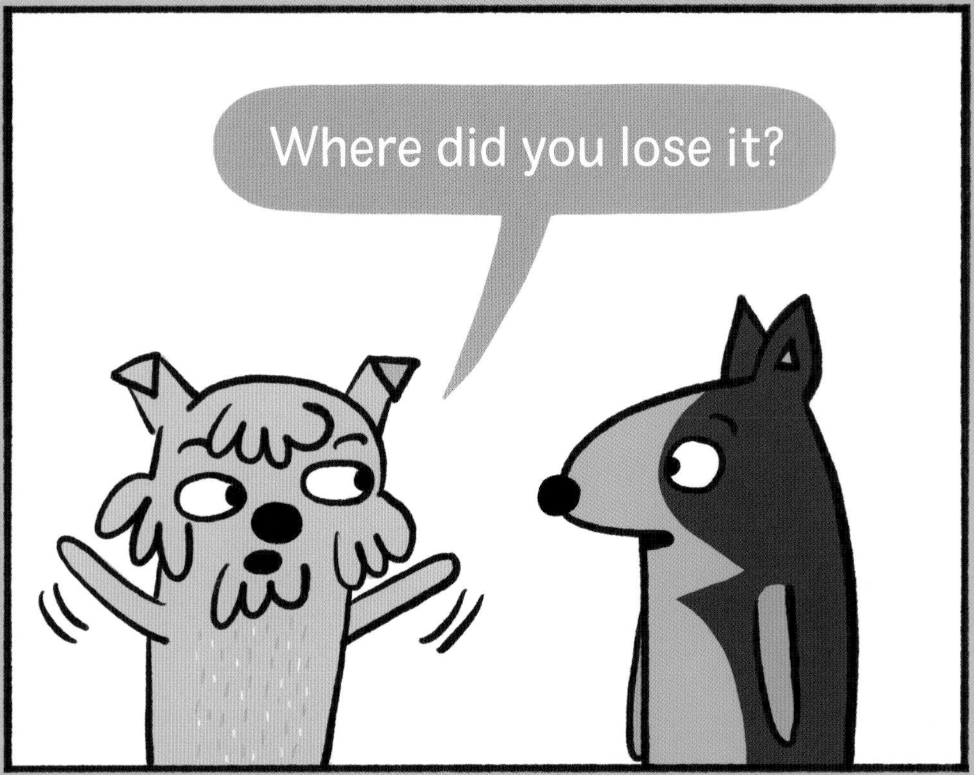
Where did you lose it?

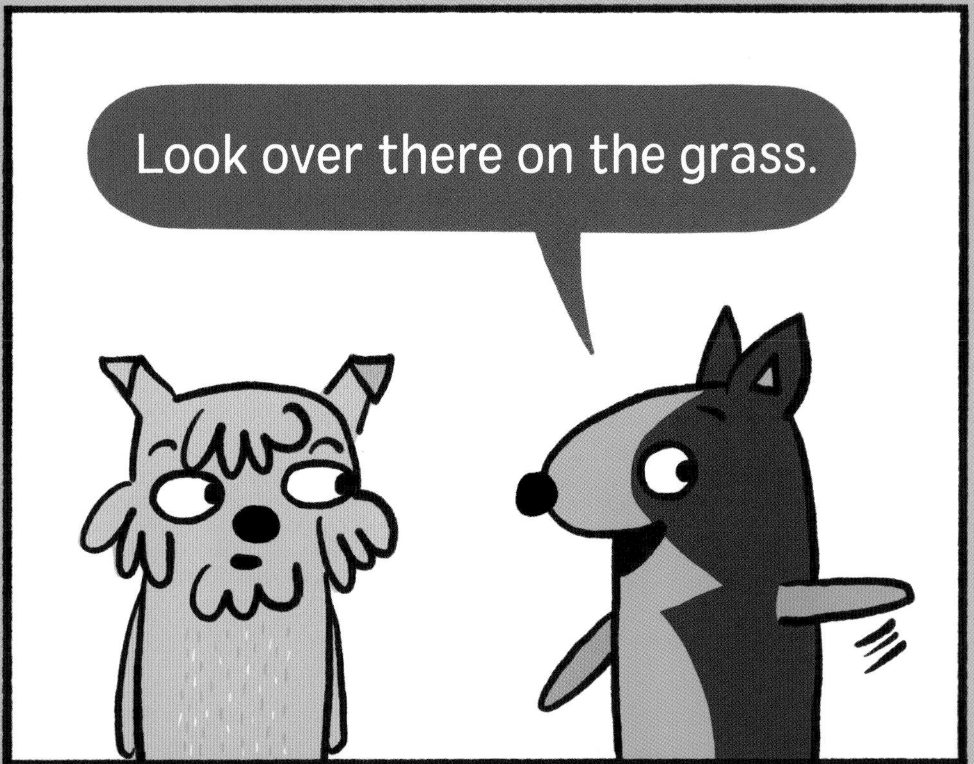
Look over there on the grass.

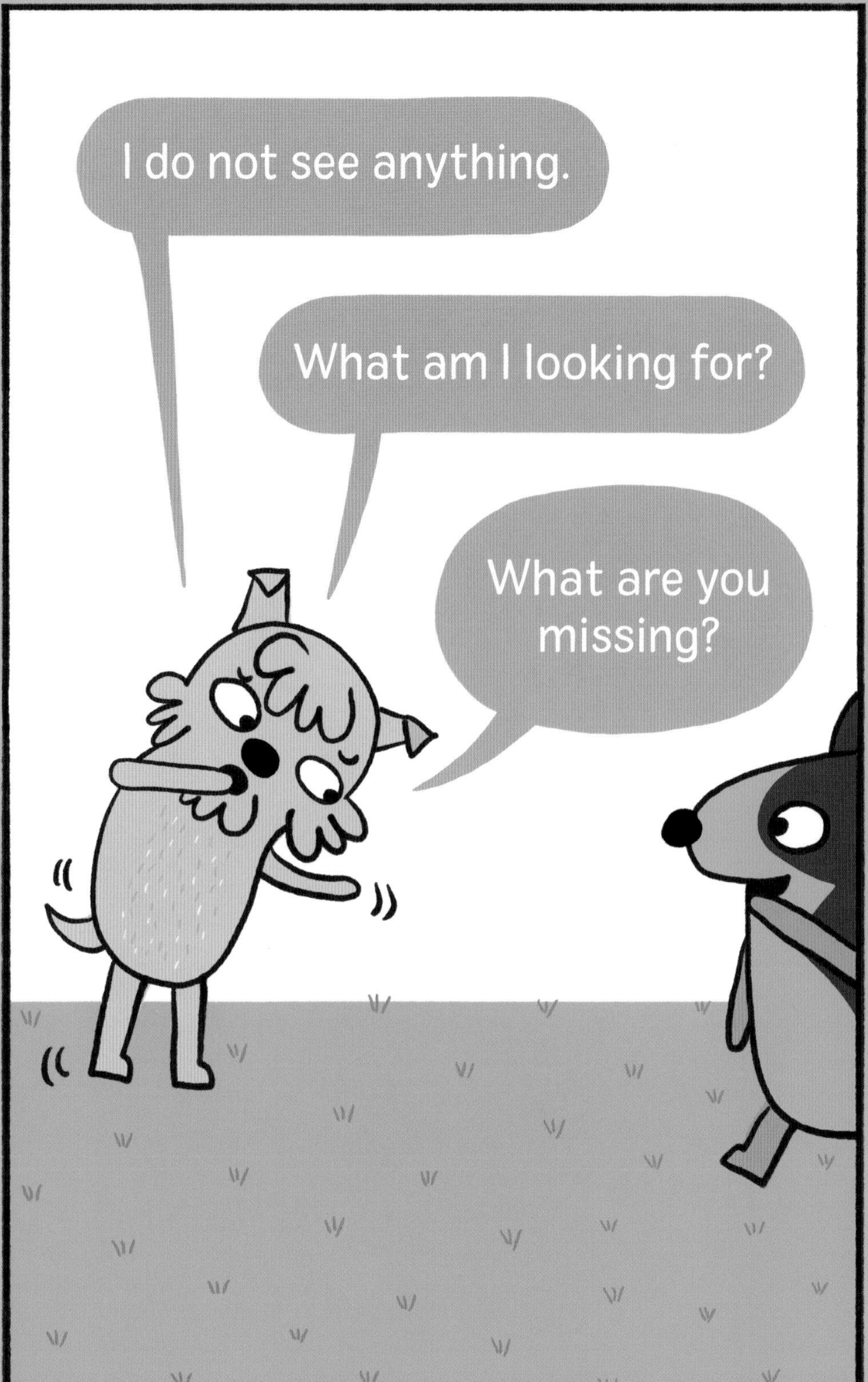
I do not see anything.
What am I looking for?
What are you missing?

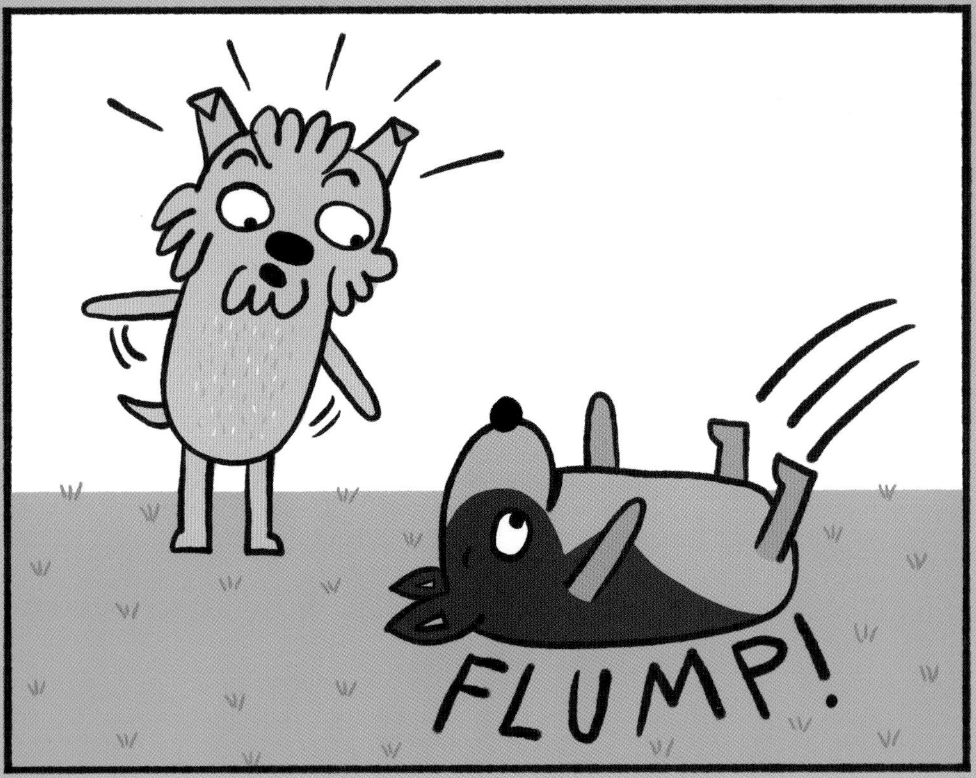
FLUMP!

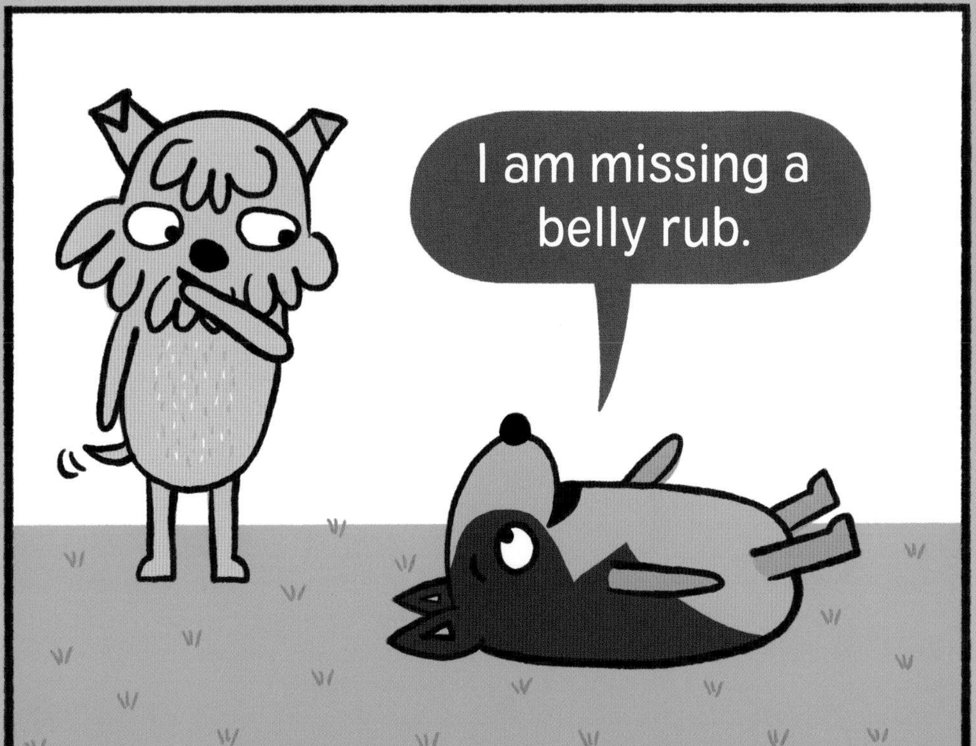
I am missing a belly rub.

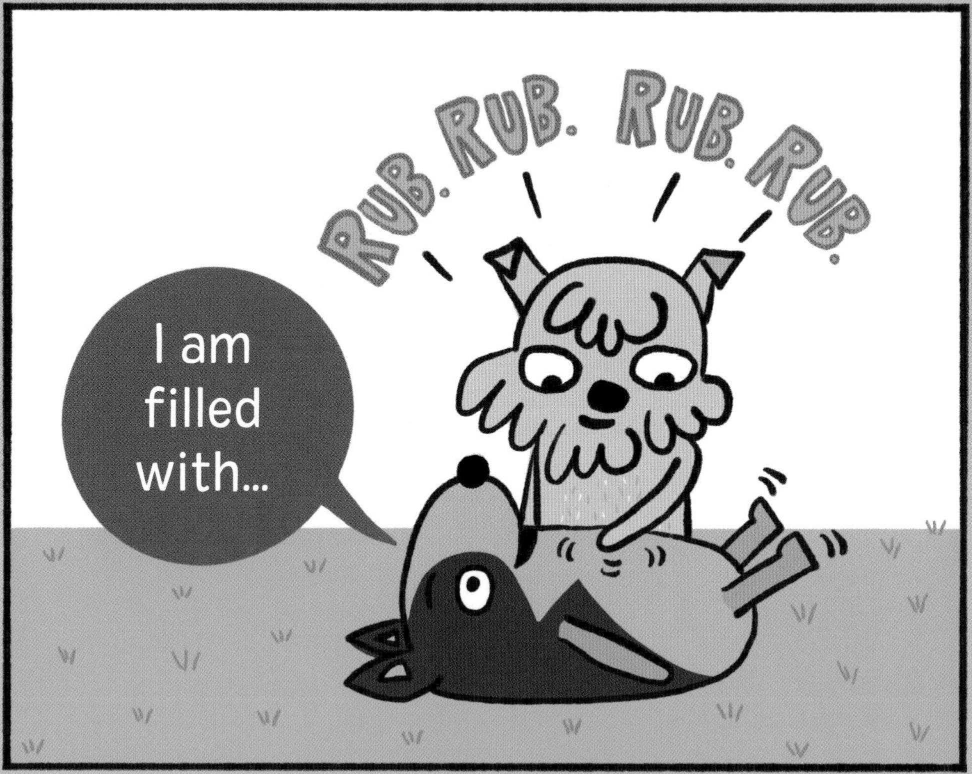
RUB. RUB. RUB. RUB.
I am filled with...

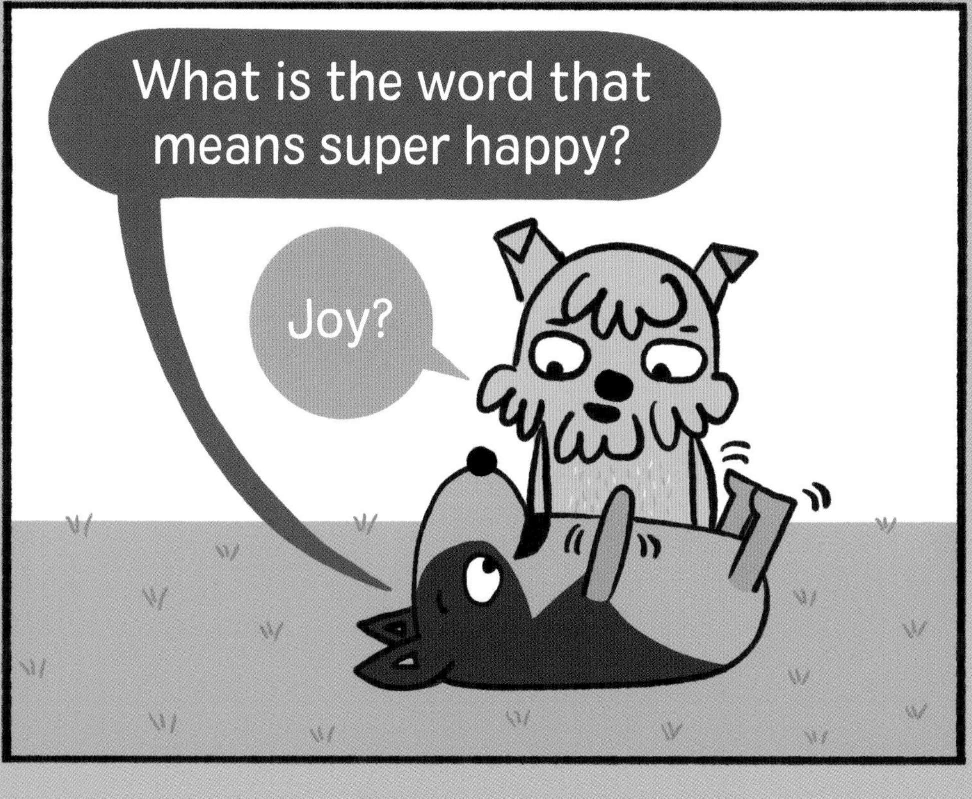
What is the word that means super happy?
Joy?

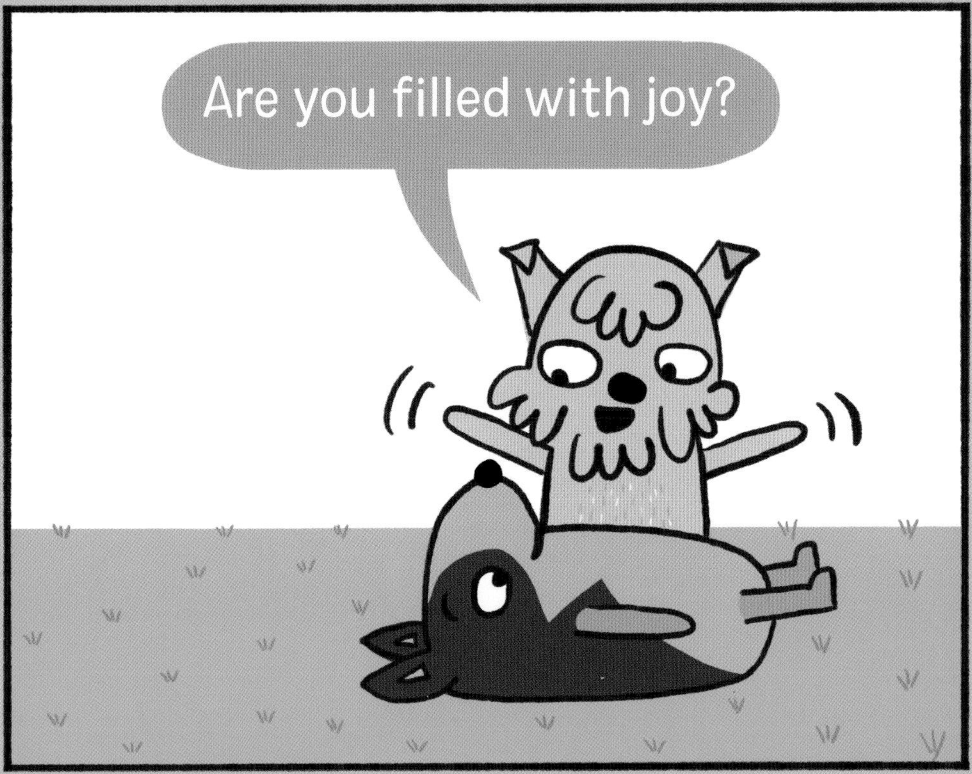
Are you filled with joy?

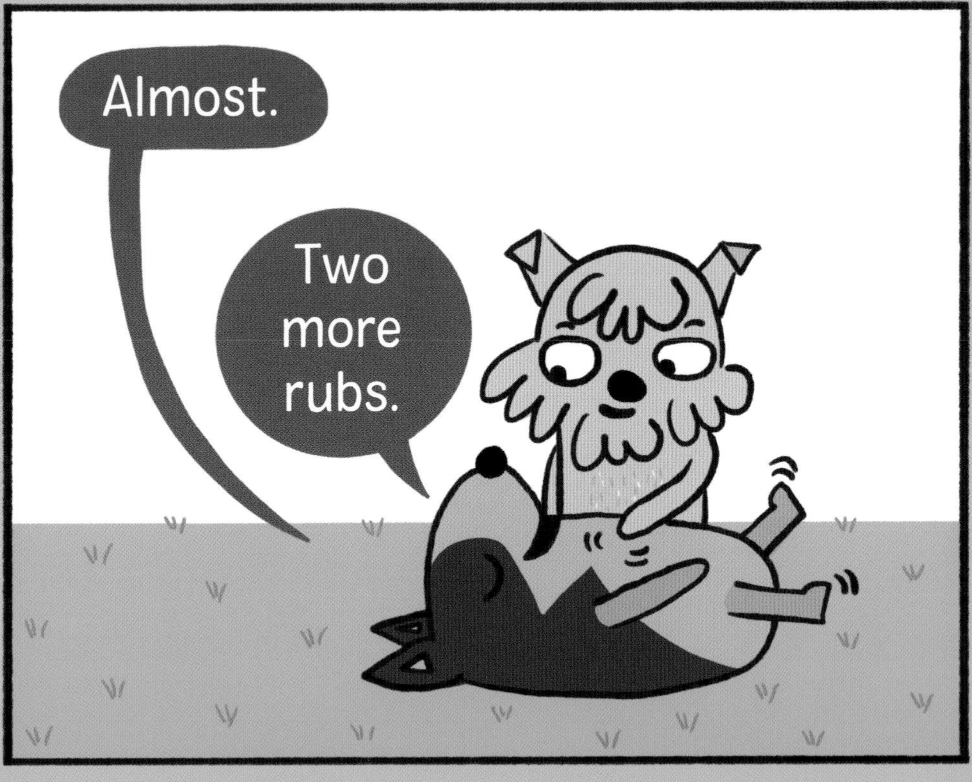
Almost.
Two more rubs.

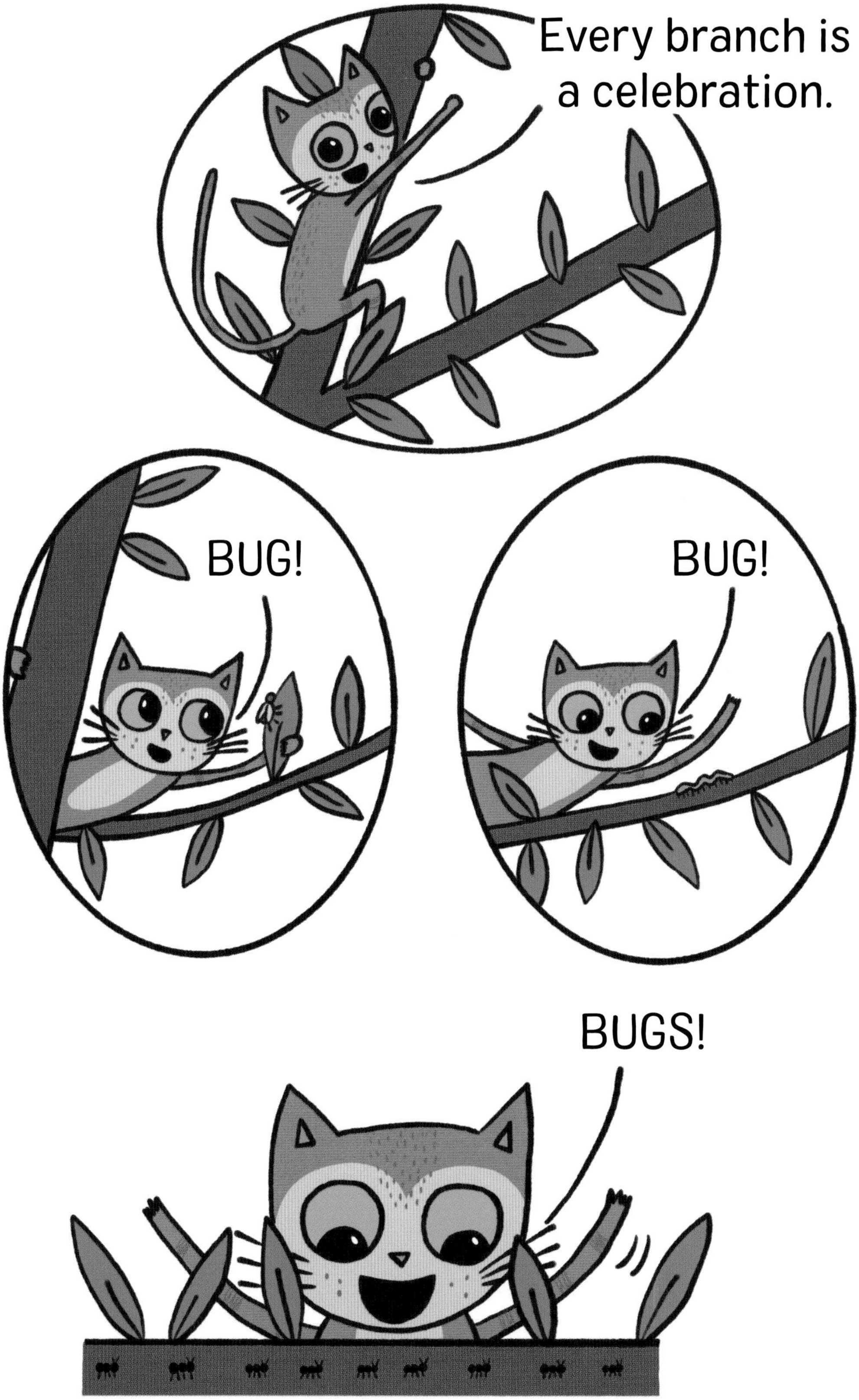
Every branch is
a celebration.
BUG!
BUG!
BUGS!

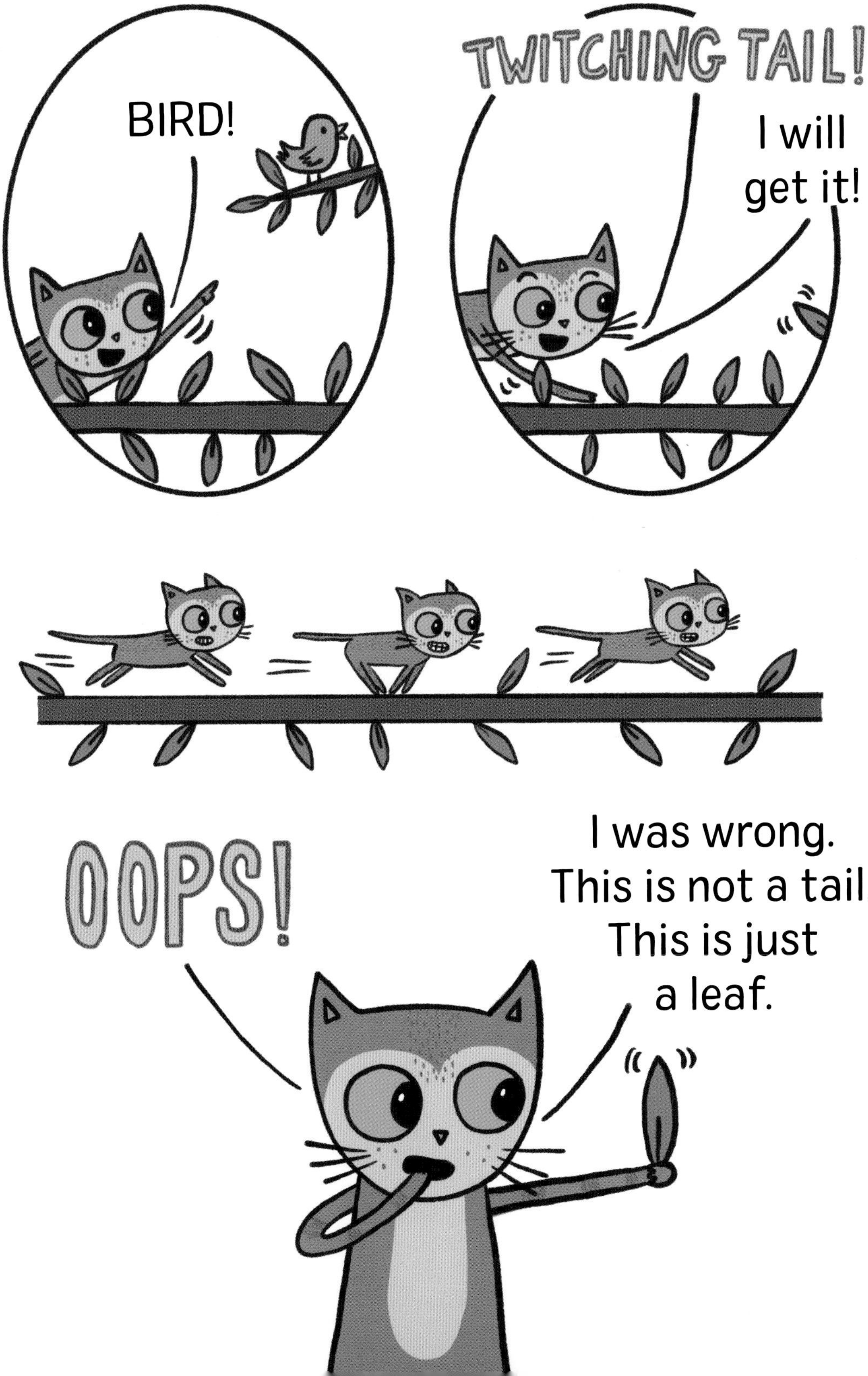
BIRD!
TWITCHING TAIL!
I will get it!
OOPS!
I was wrong. This is not a tail. This is just a leaf.

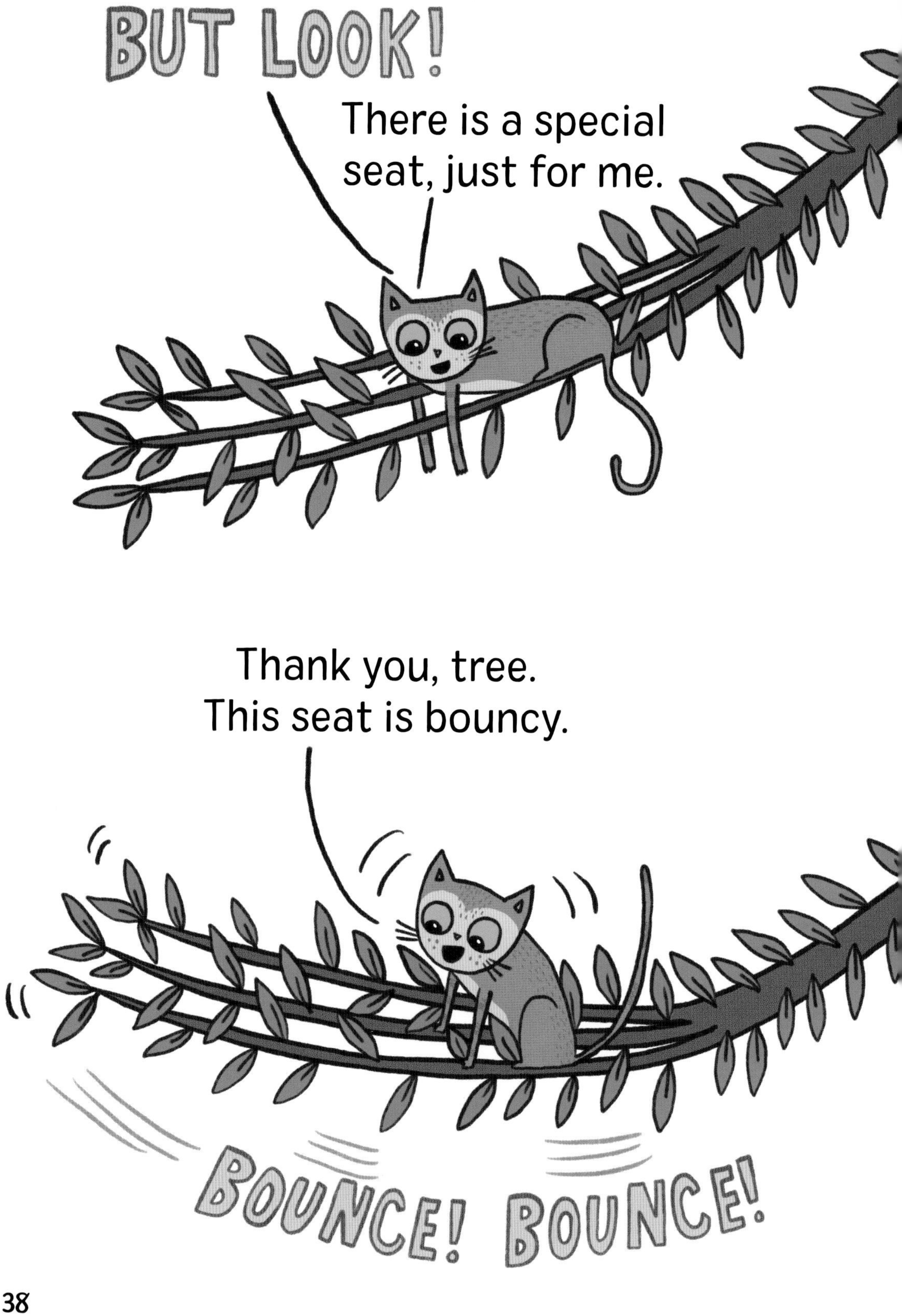
BUT LOOK!
There is a special seat, just for me.
Thank you, tree. This seat is bouncy.
BOUNCE! BOUNCE!

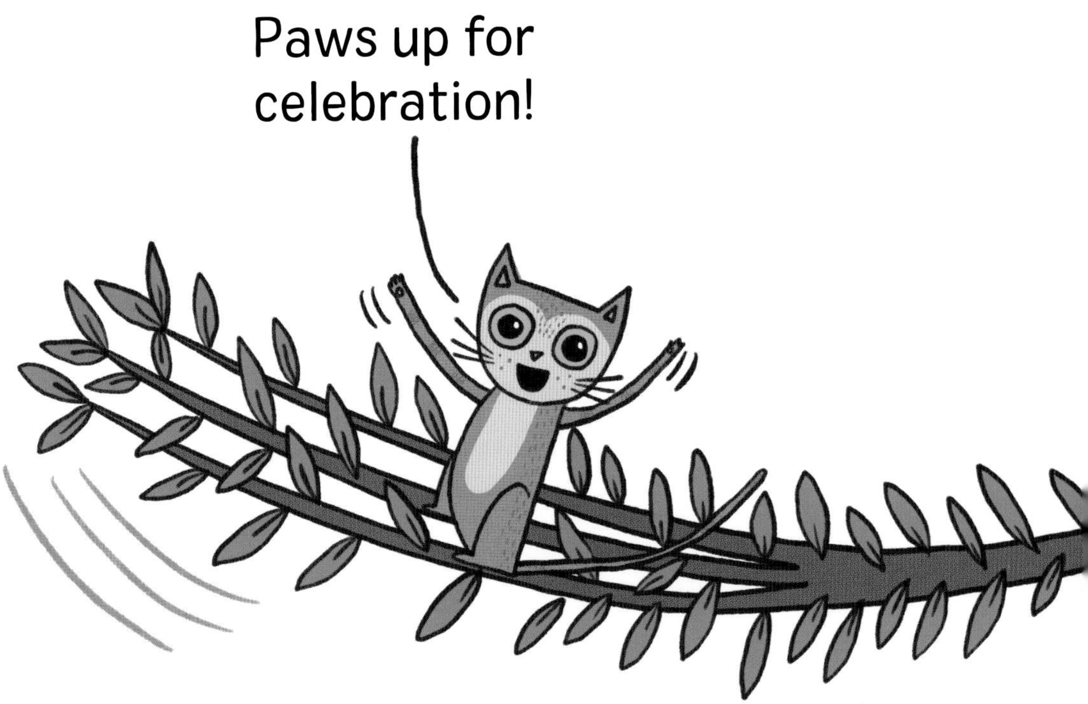
Paws up for
celebration!

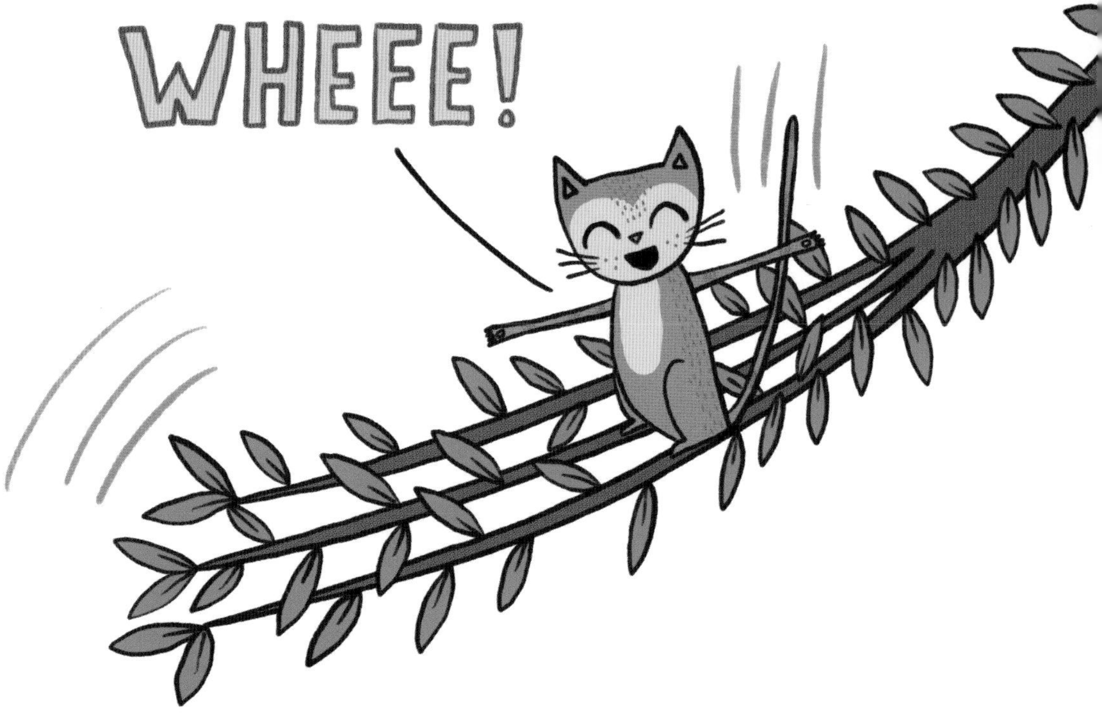
WHEEE!

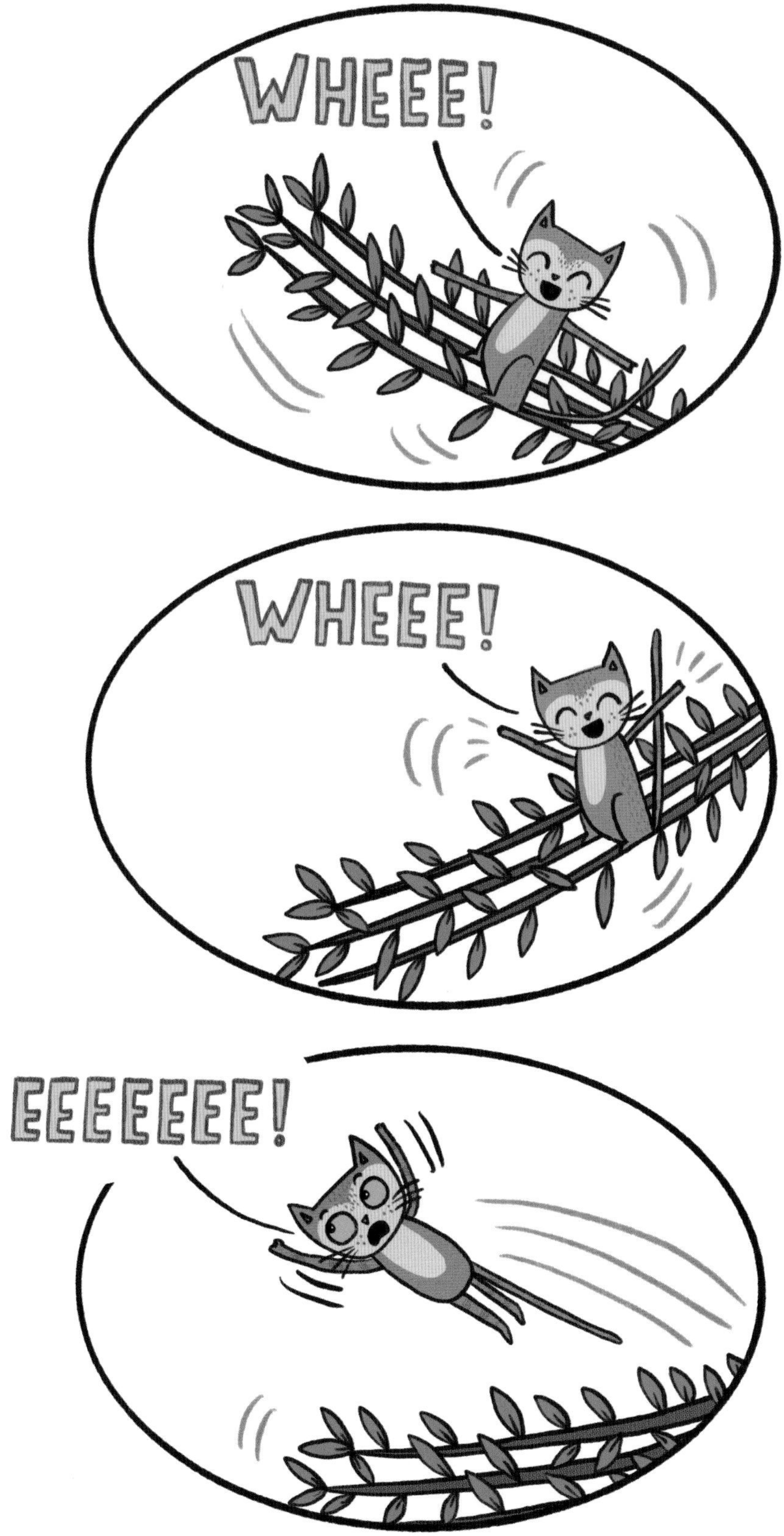
WHEEE!
WHEEE!
EEEEEEE!

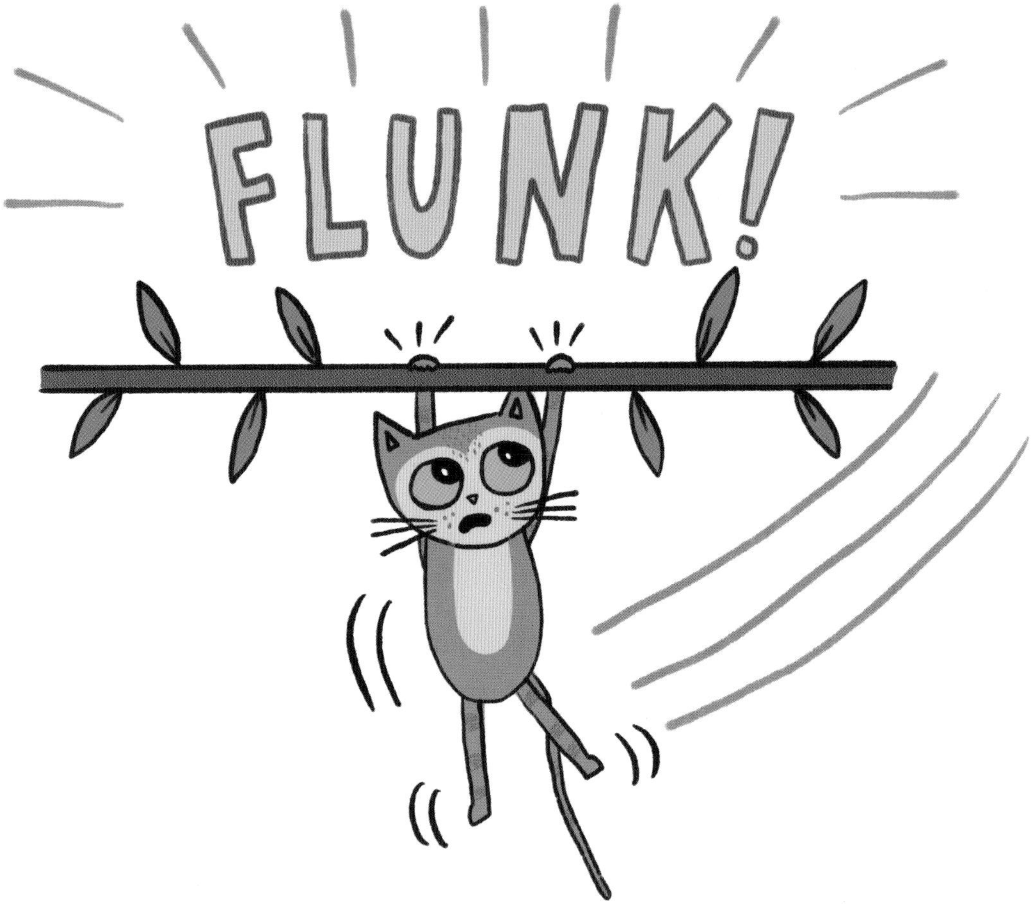
FLUNK!

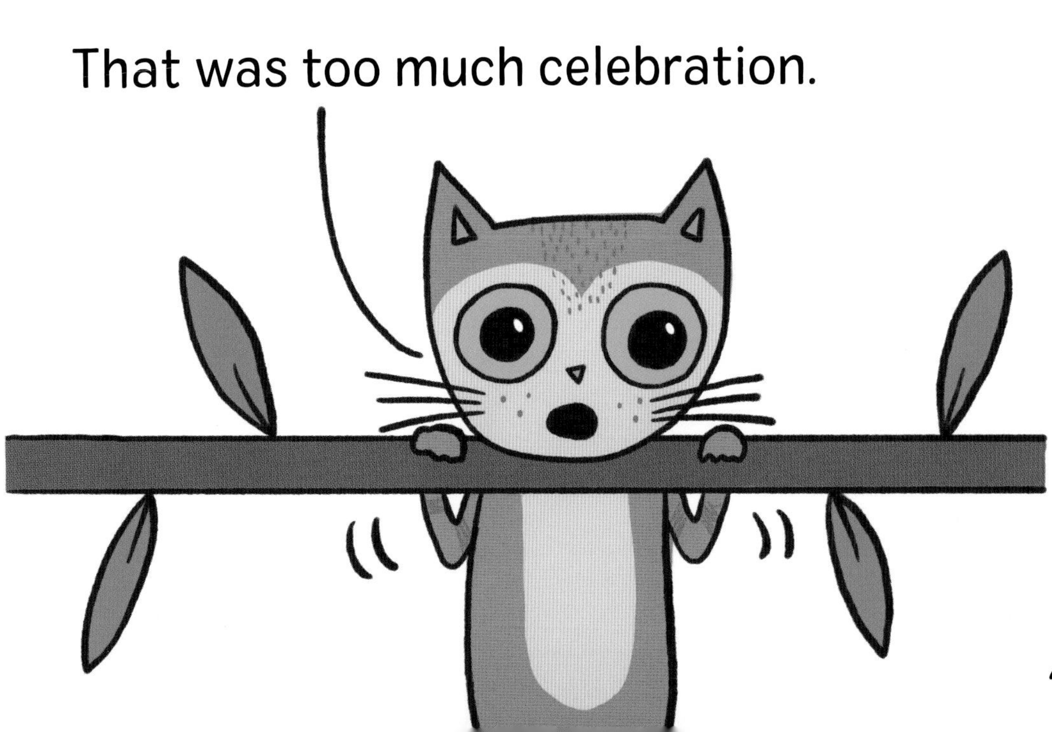
That was too much celebration.

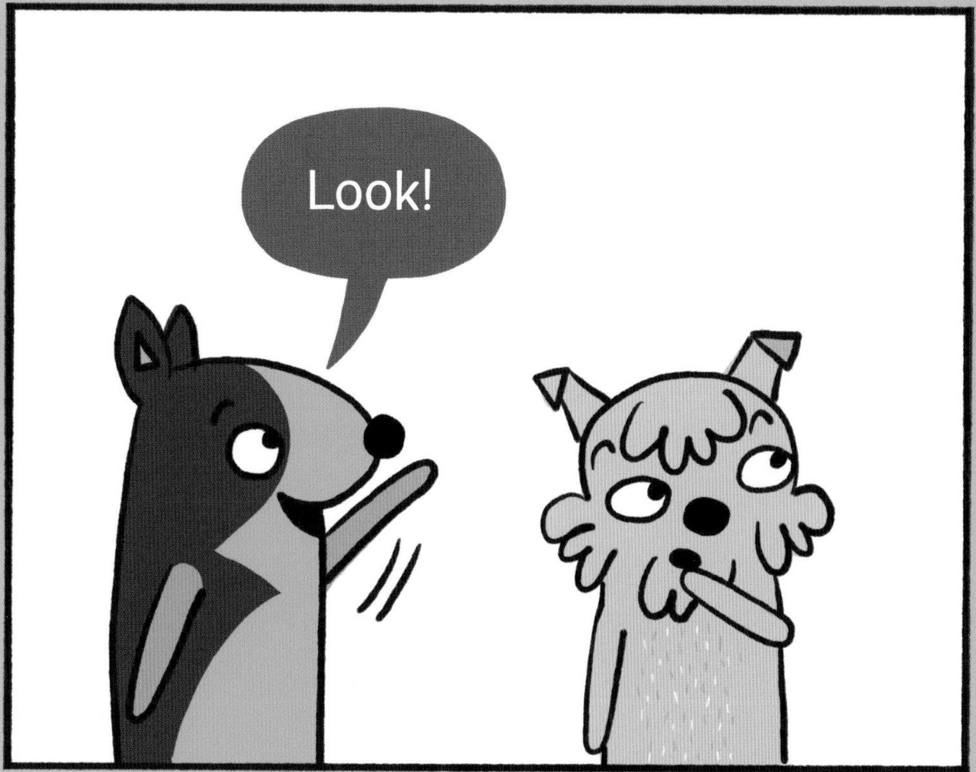
Look!

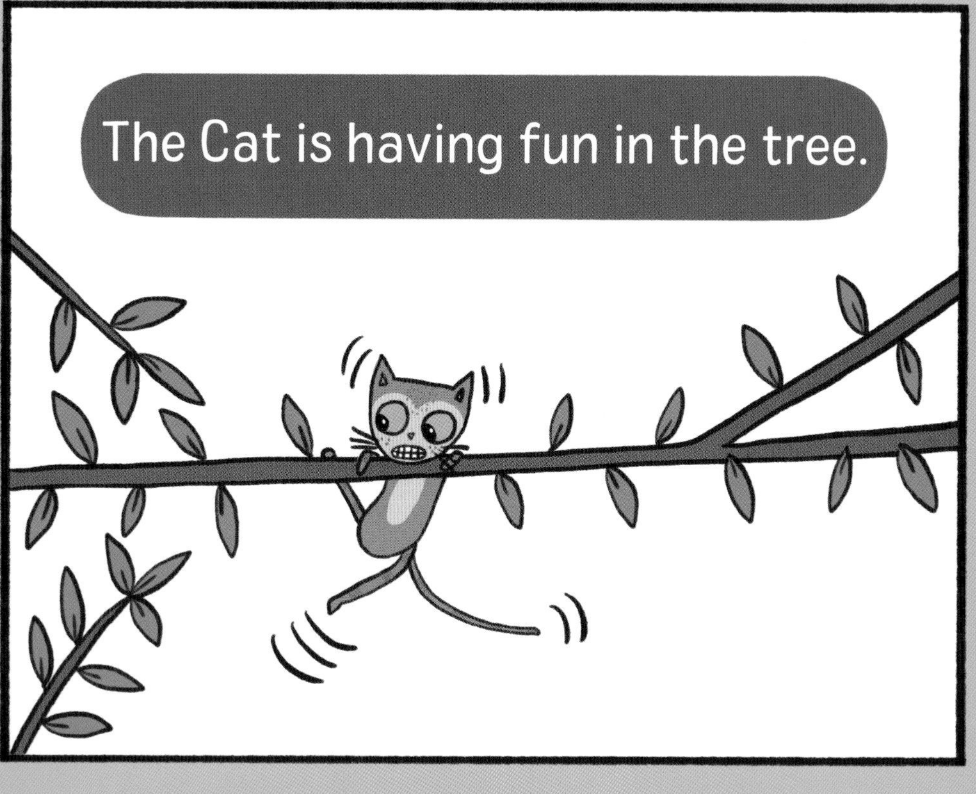
The Cat is having fun in the tree.

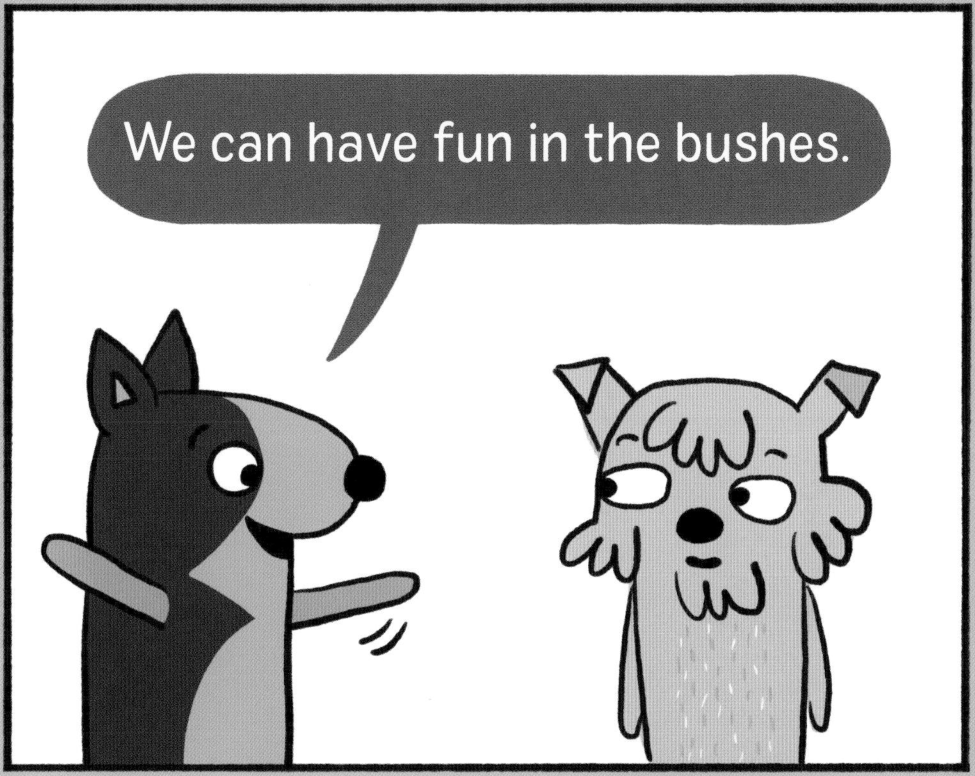
We can have fun in the bushes.

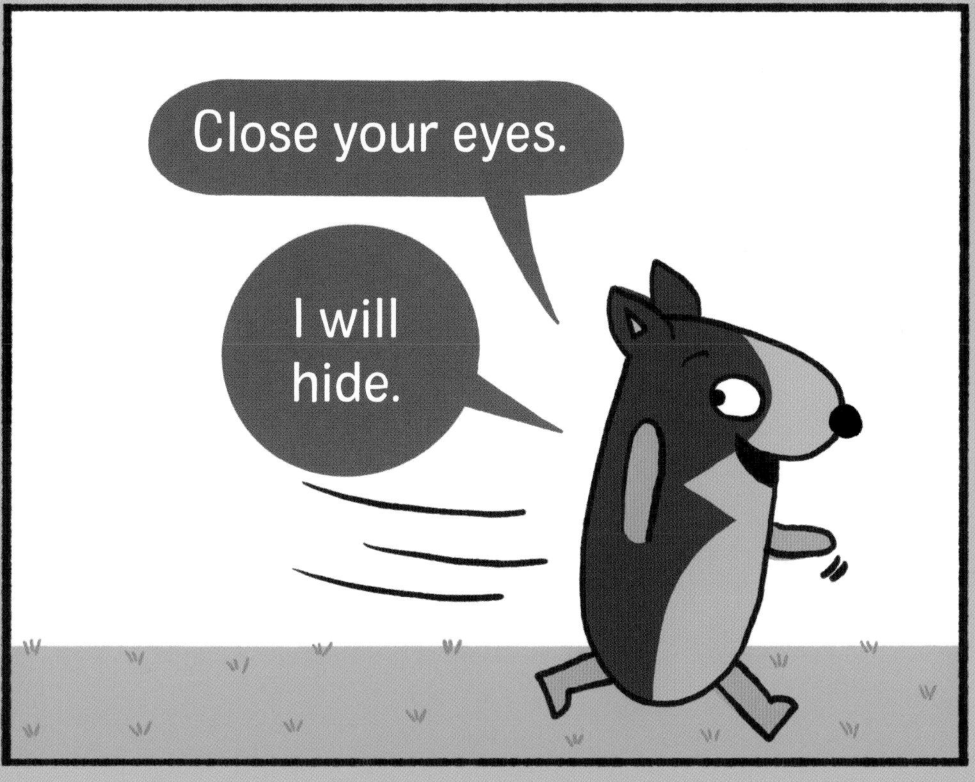
Close your eyes.
I will hide.

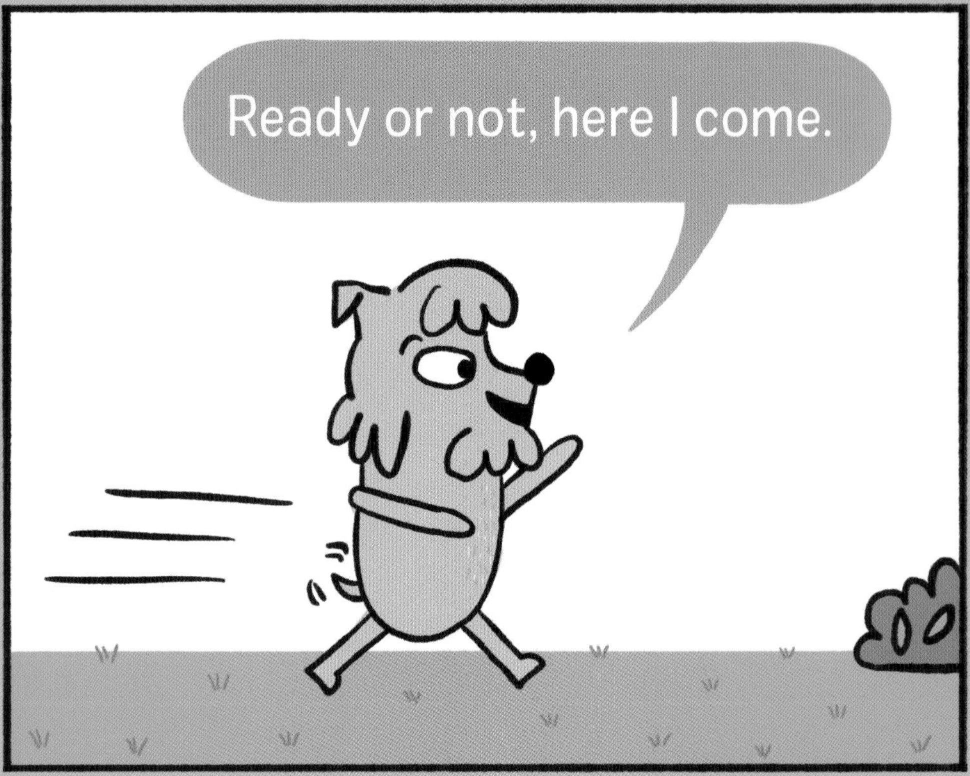
Ready or not, here I come.

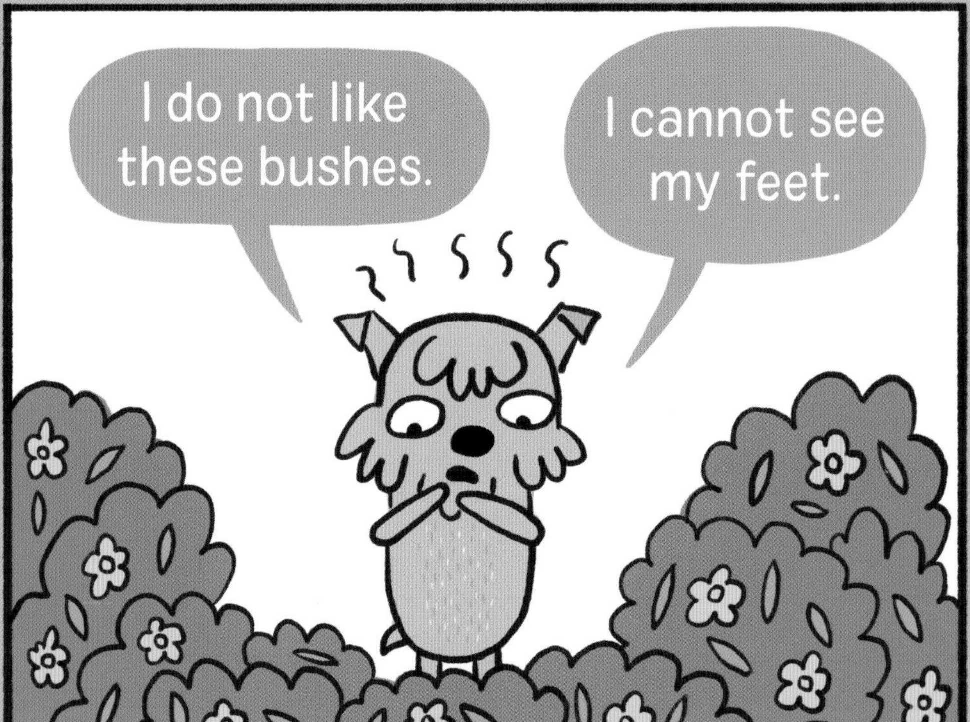
I do not like these bushes.
I cannot see my feet.

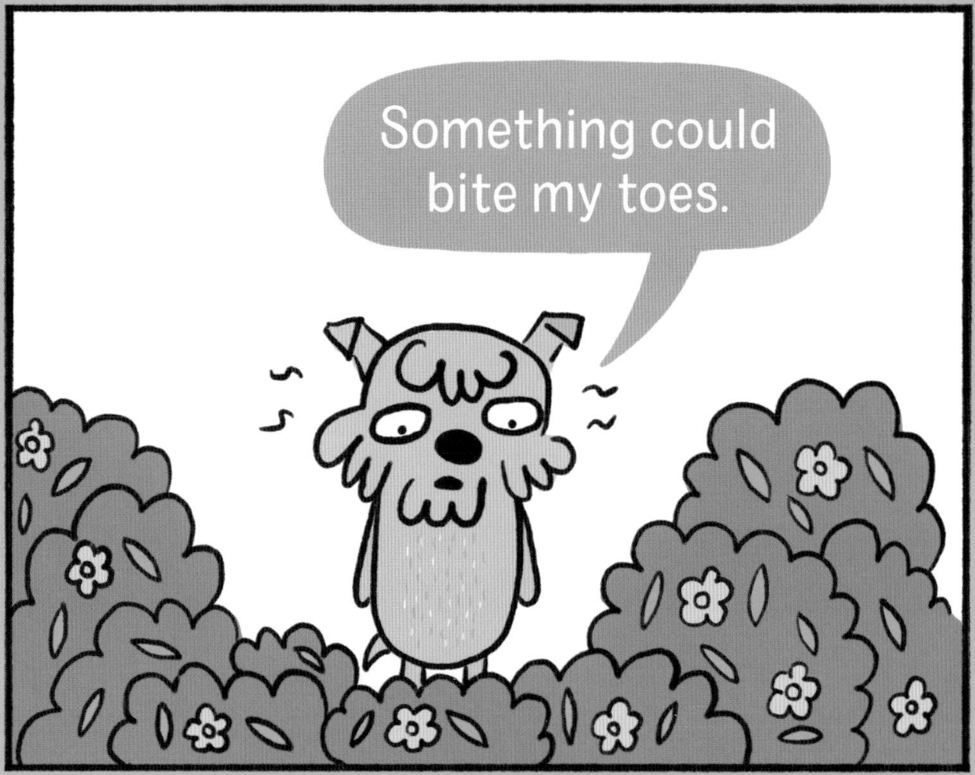
Something could bite my toes.

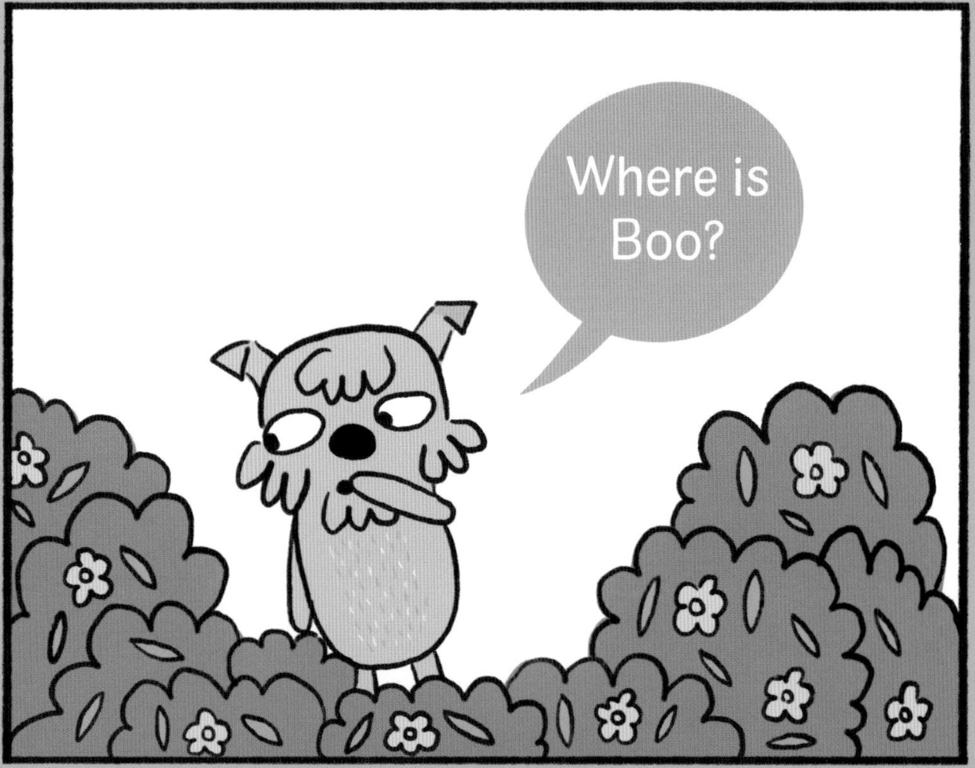
Where is Boo?

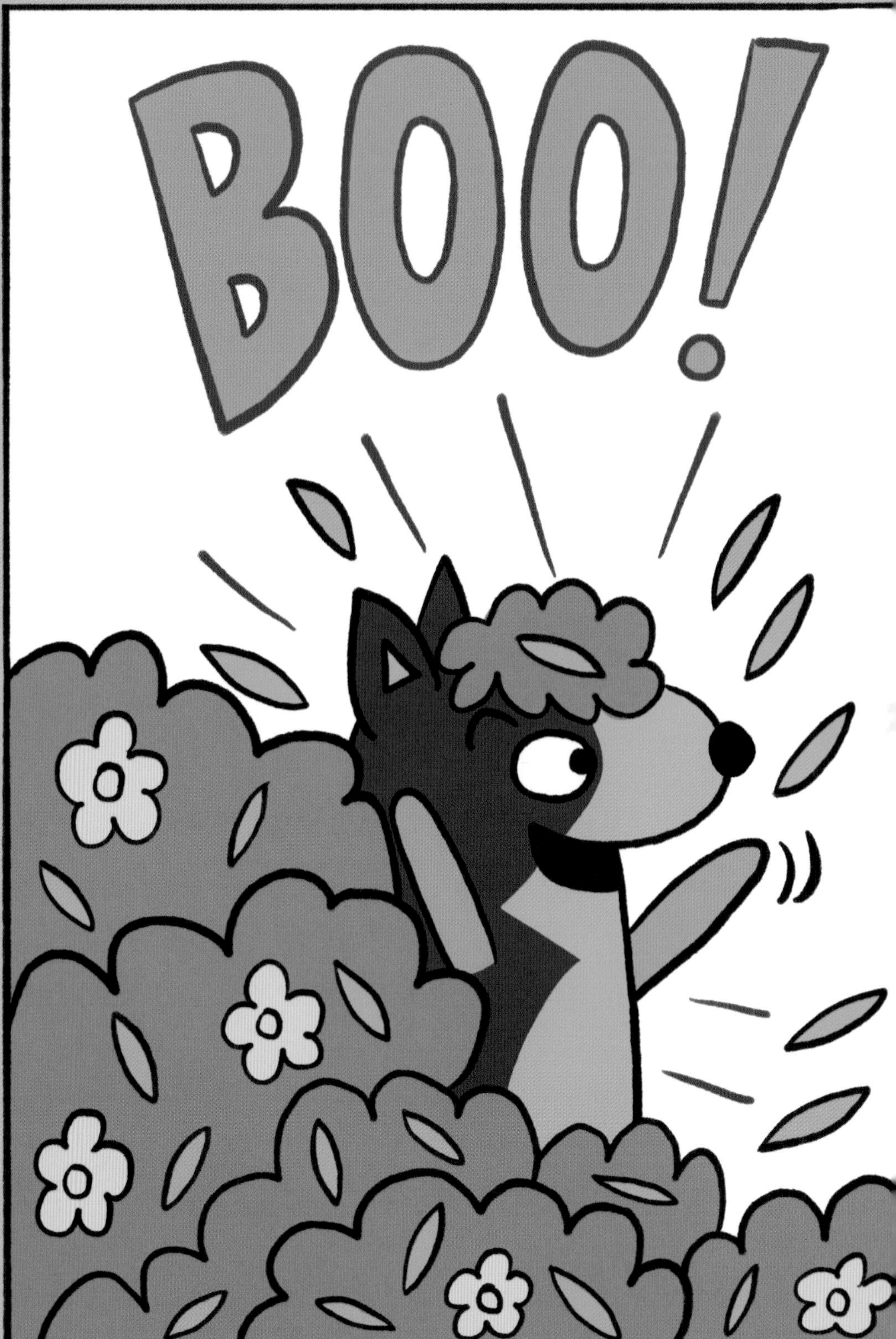
BOO!

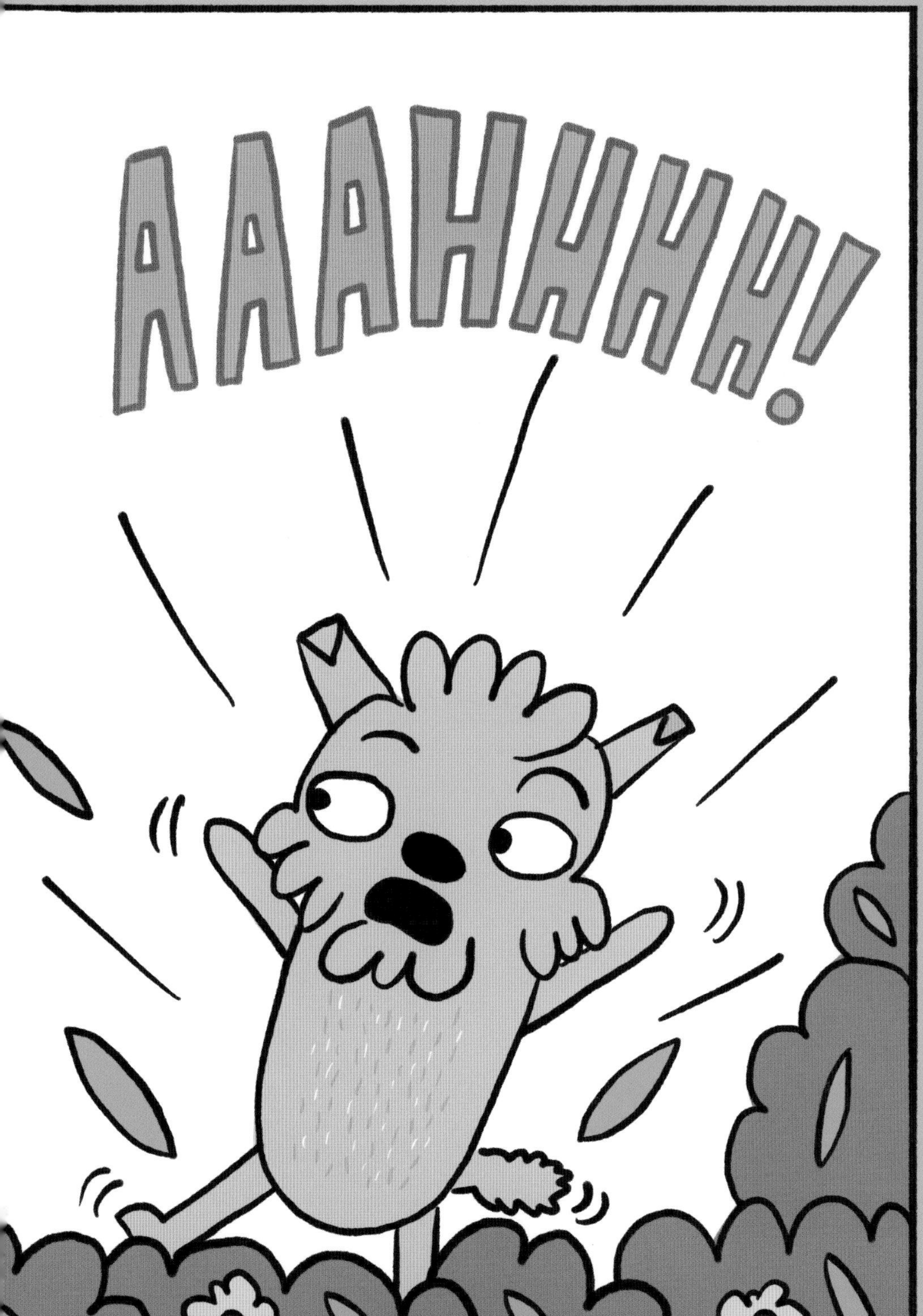
AAAHHHH!

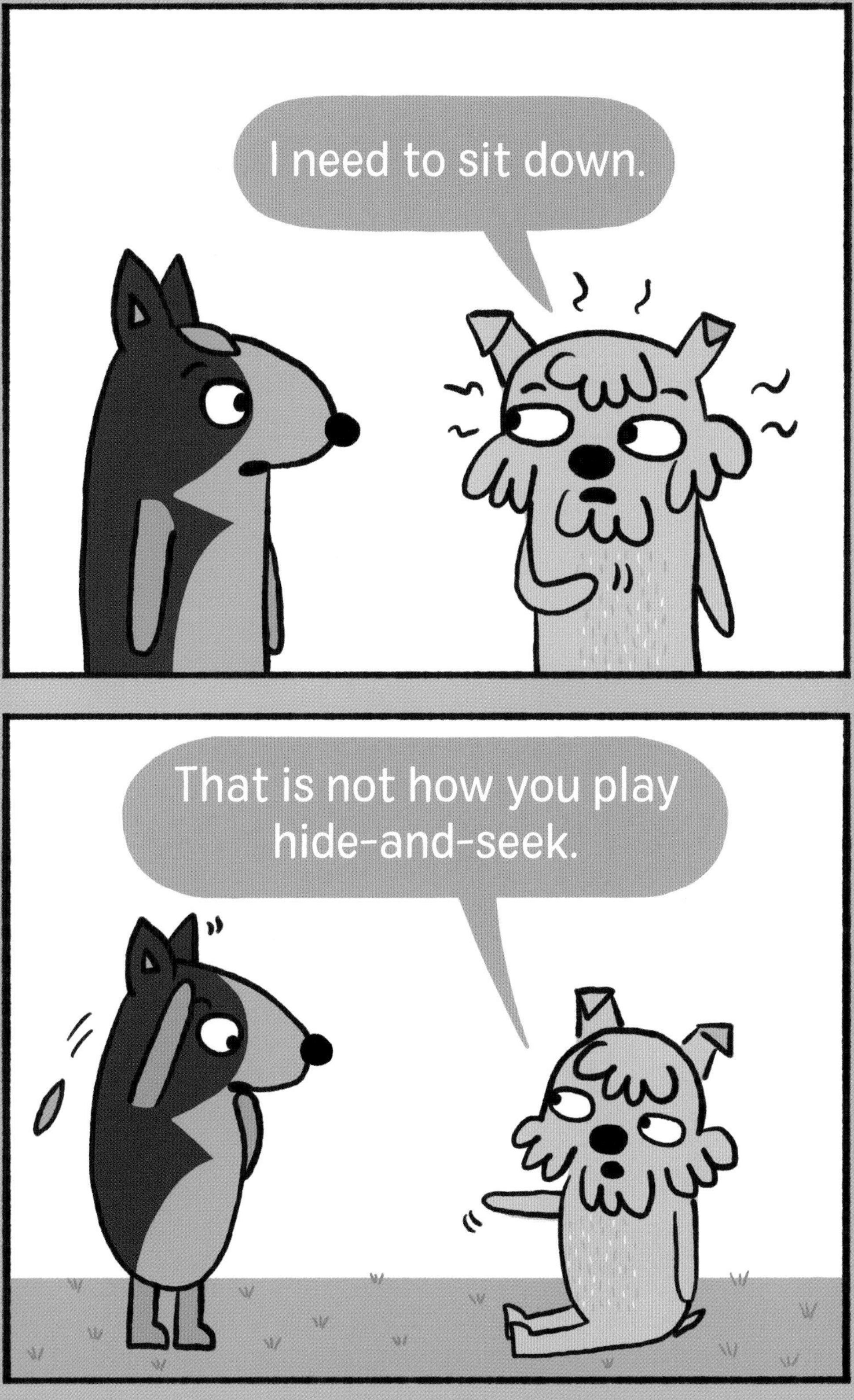
I need to sit down.
That is not how you play hide-and-seek.

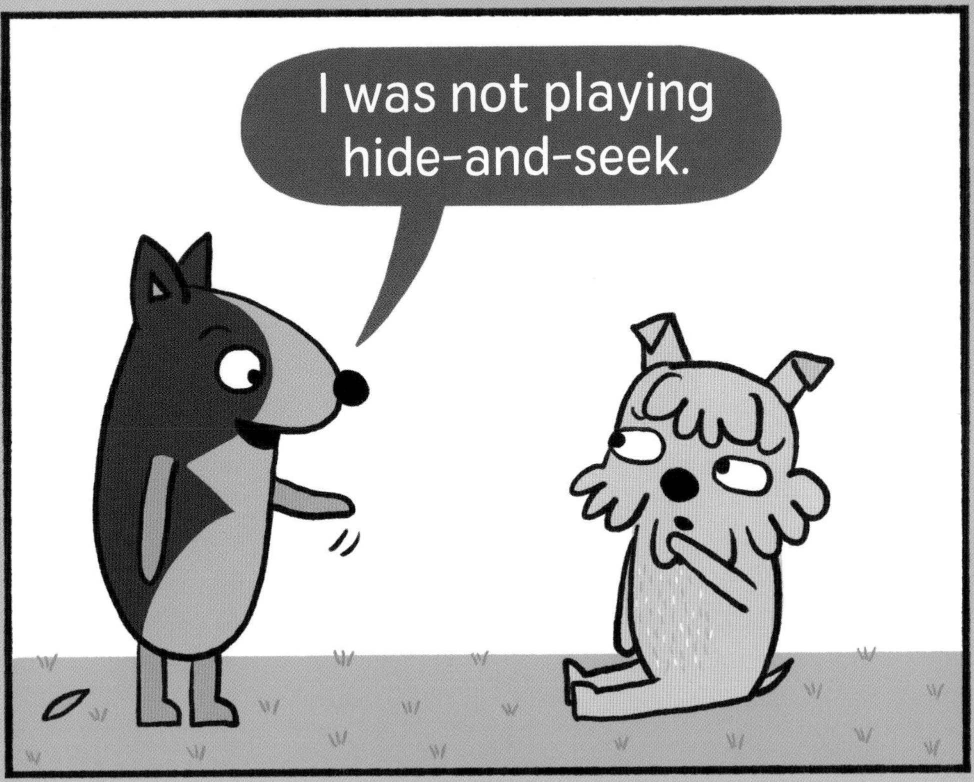
I was not playing hide-and-seek.

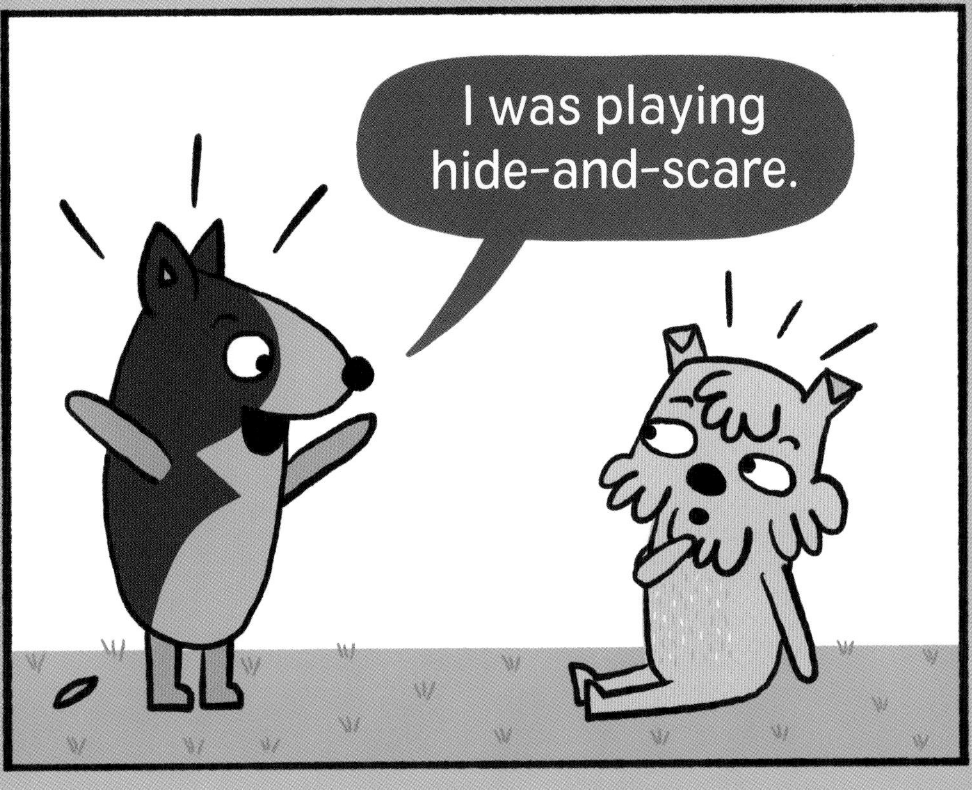
I was playing hide-and-scare.

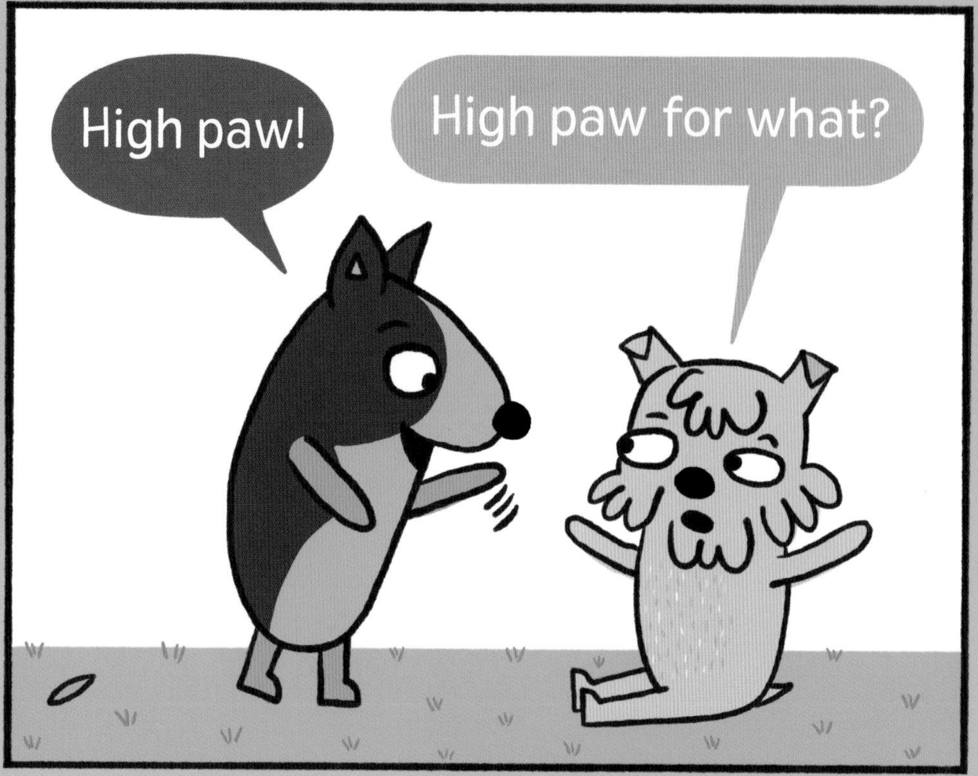
High paw!
High paw for what?

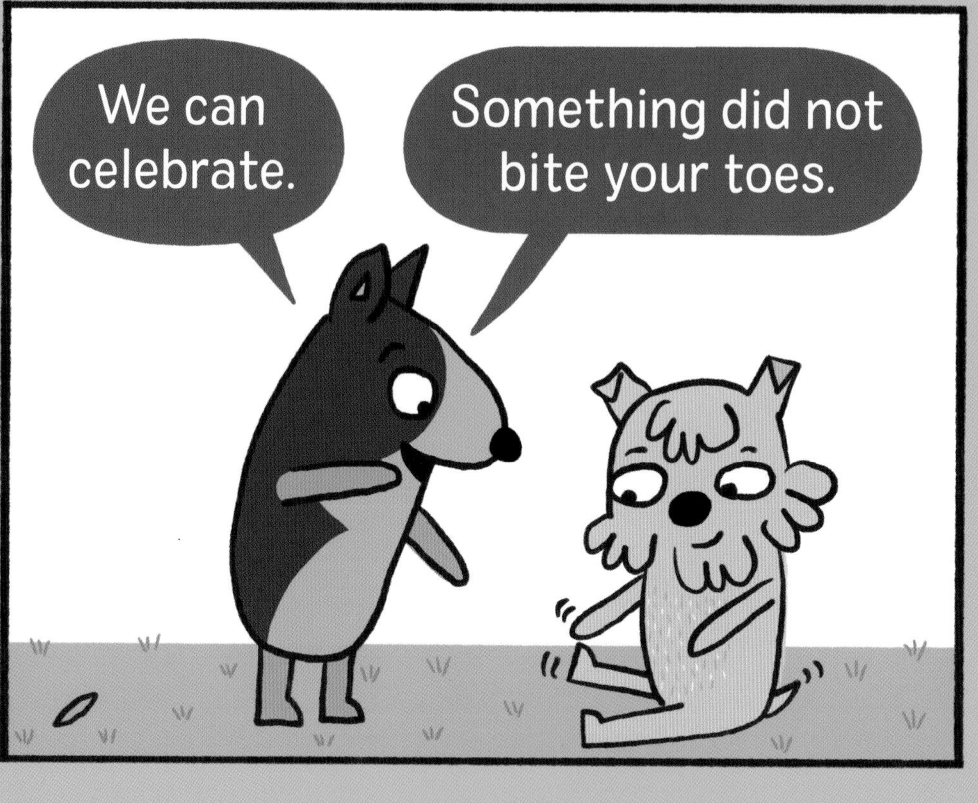
We can celebrate.
Something did not bite your toes.

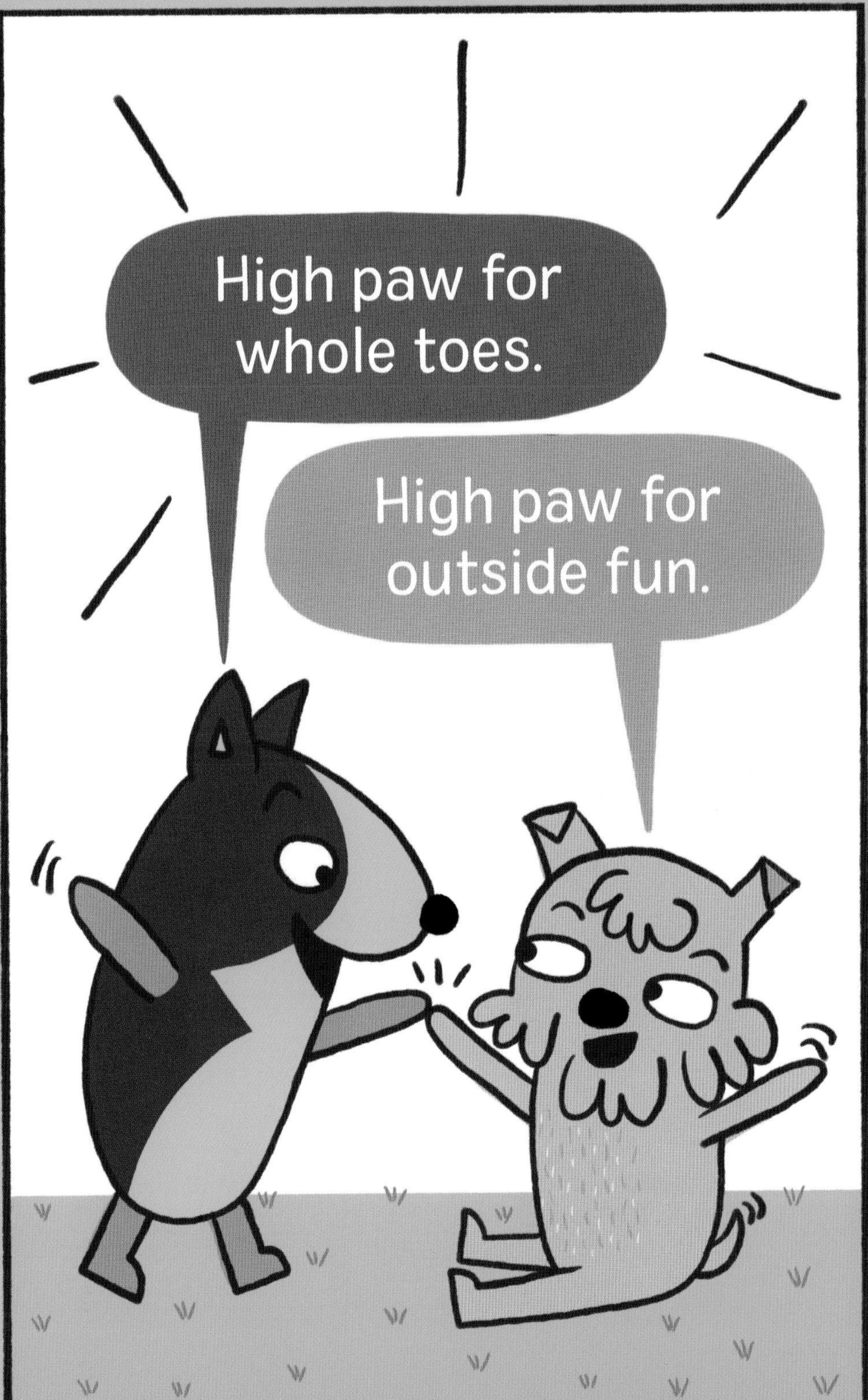
High paw for whole toes.
High paw for outside fun.

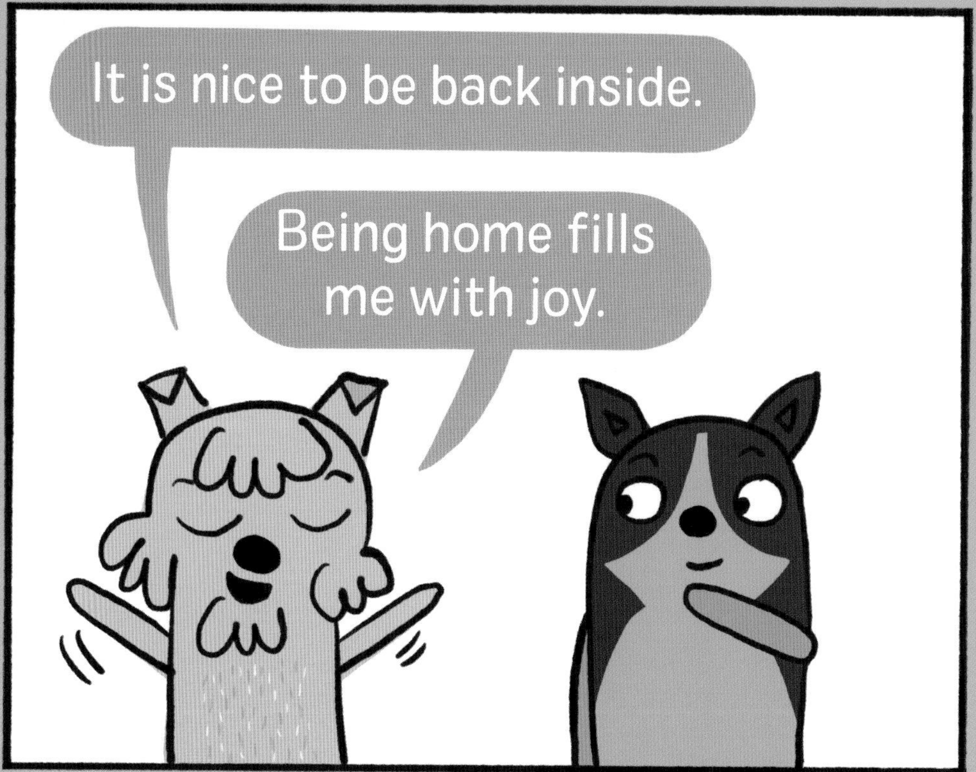
It is nice to be back inside.
Being home fills me with joy.

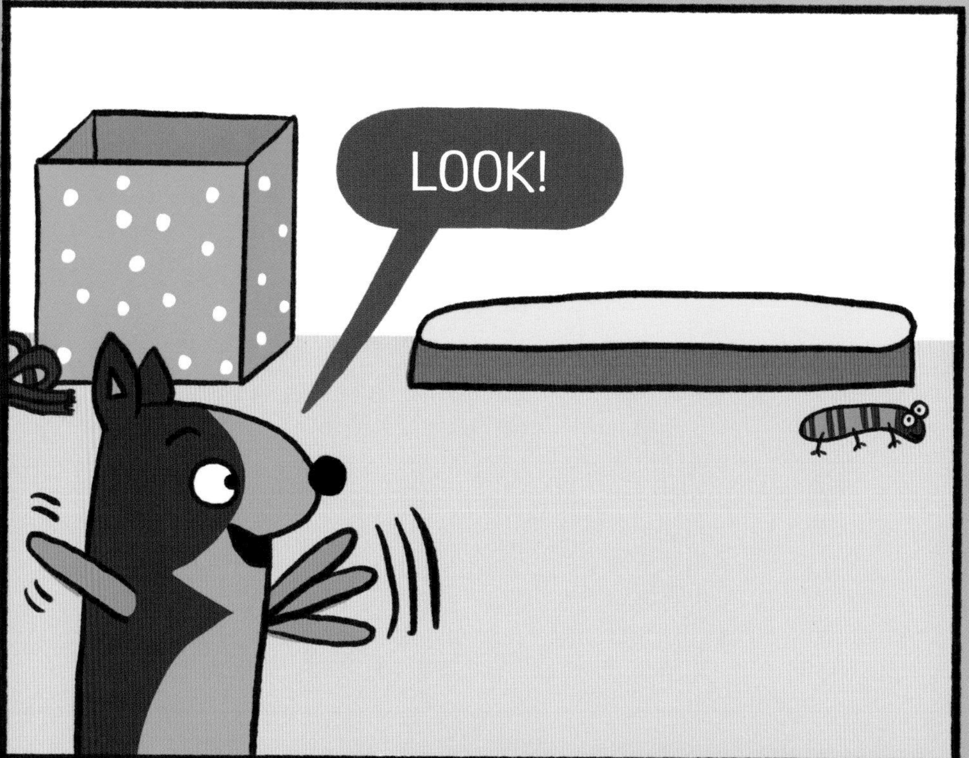
LOOK!

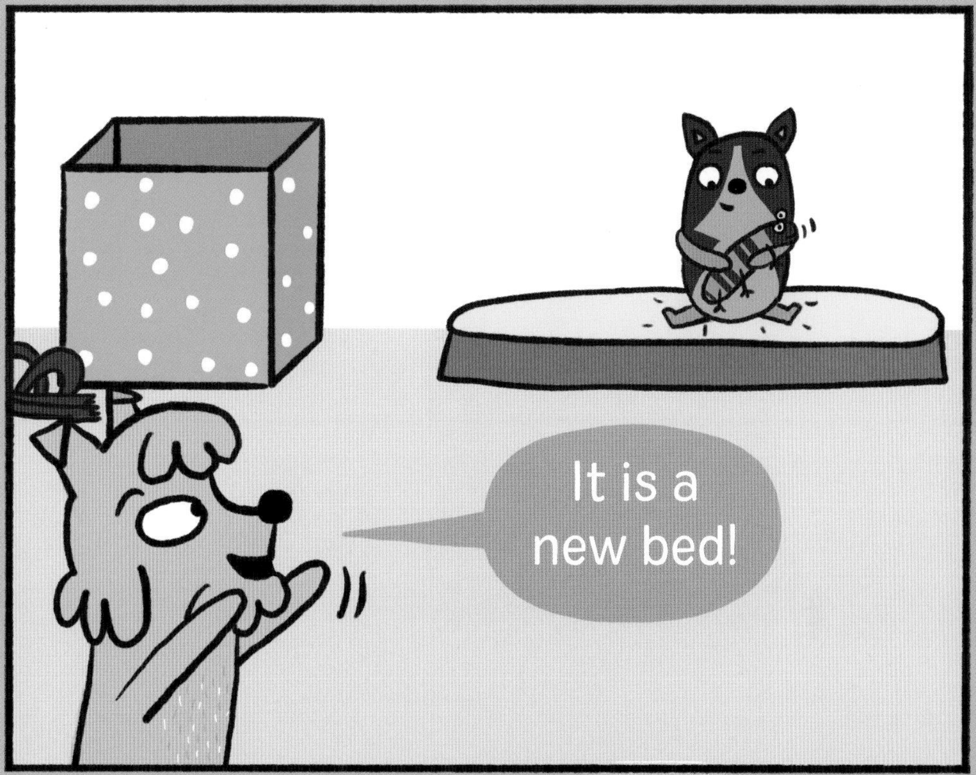
It is a
new bed!

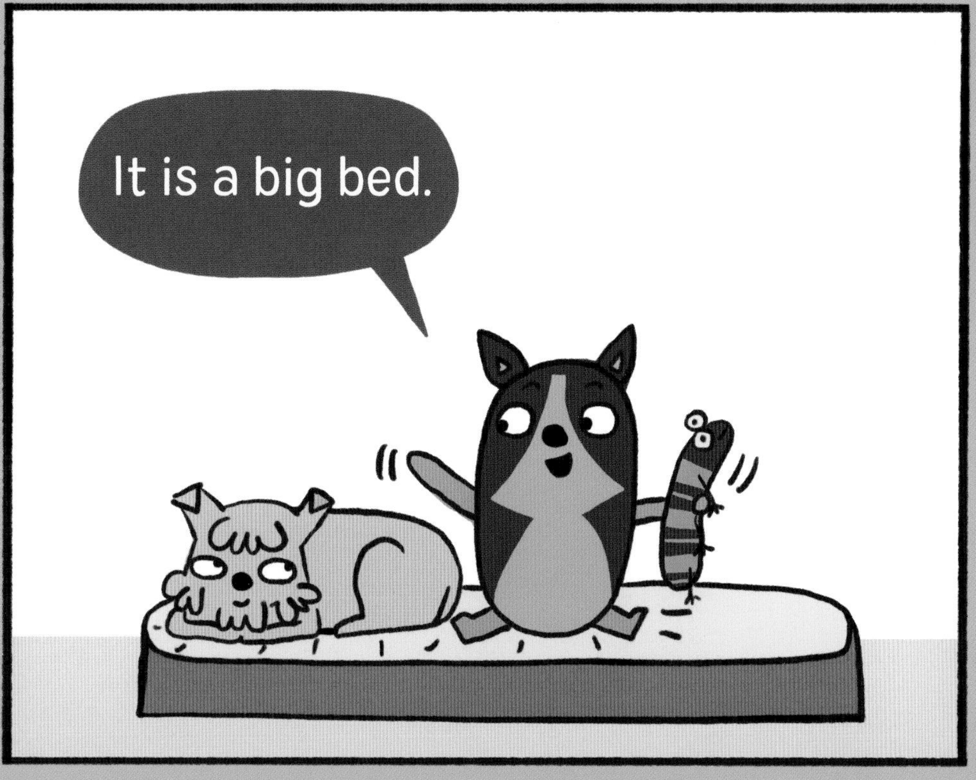
It is a big bed.

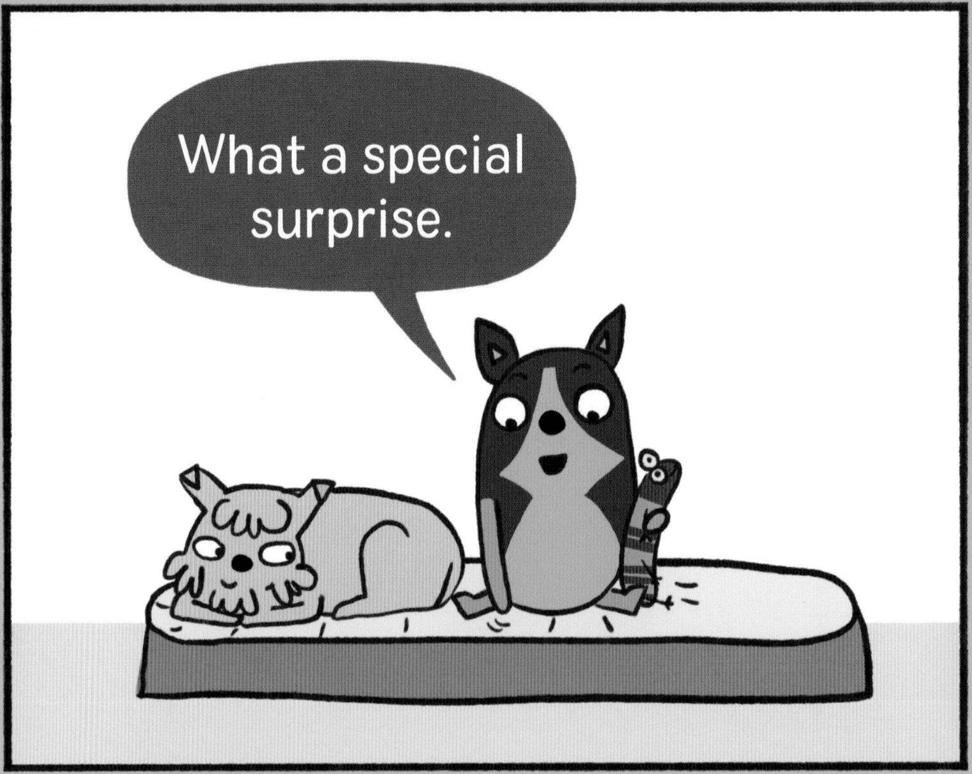
What a special surprise.

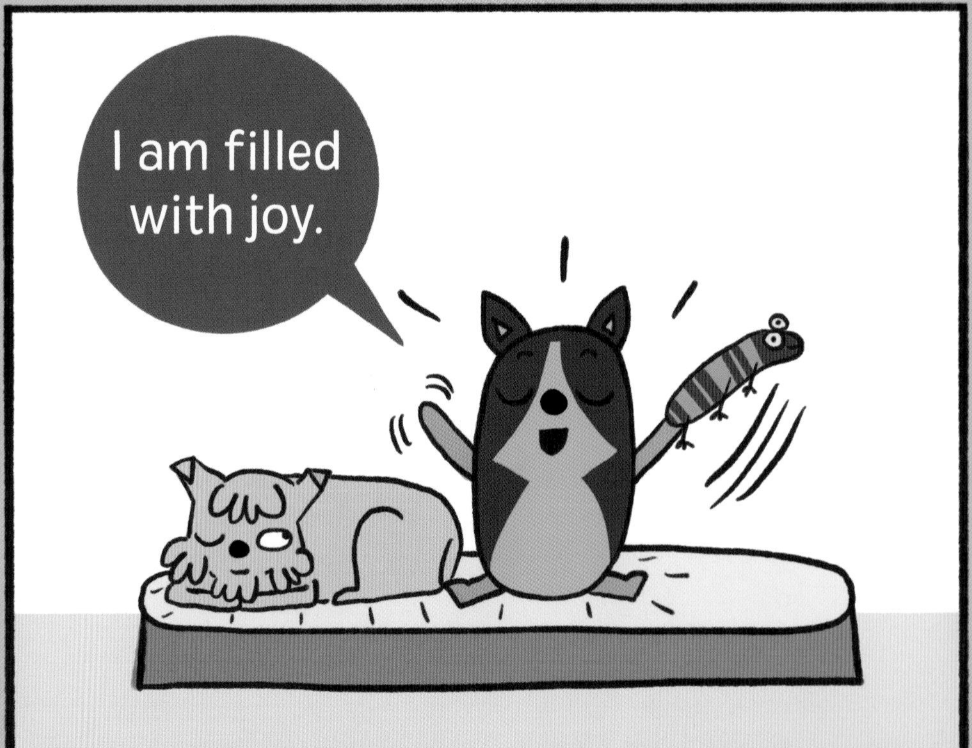
I am filled with joy.

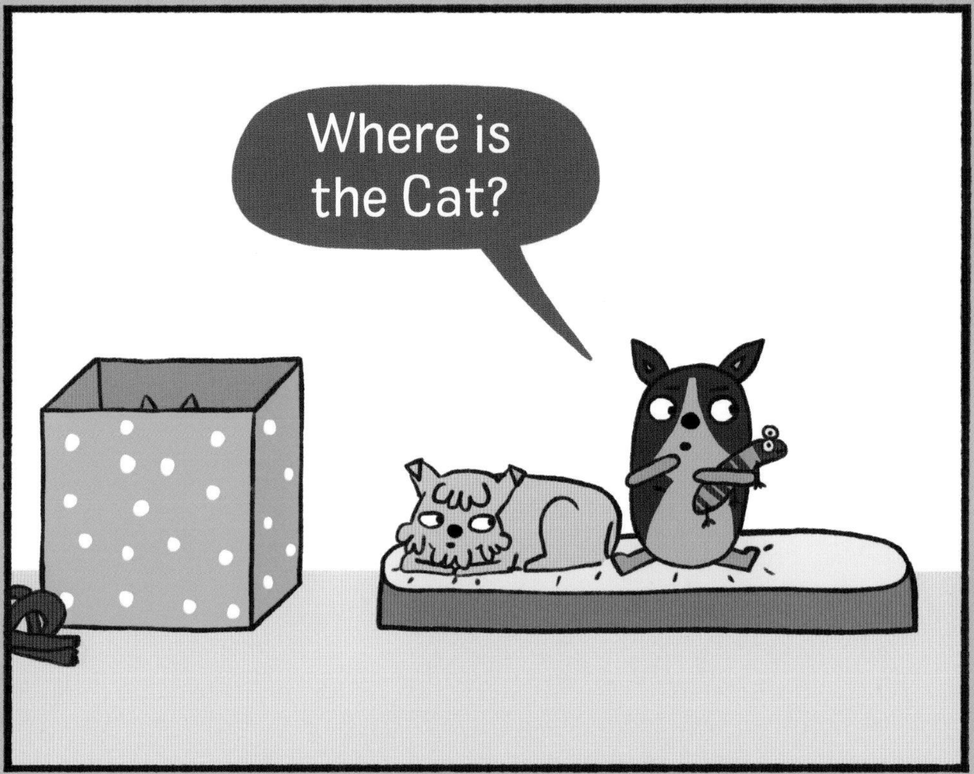
Where is the Cat?

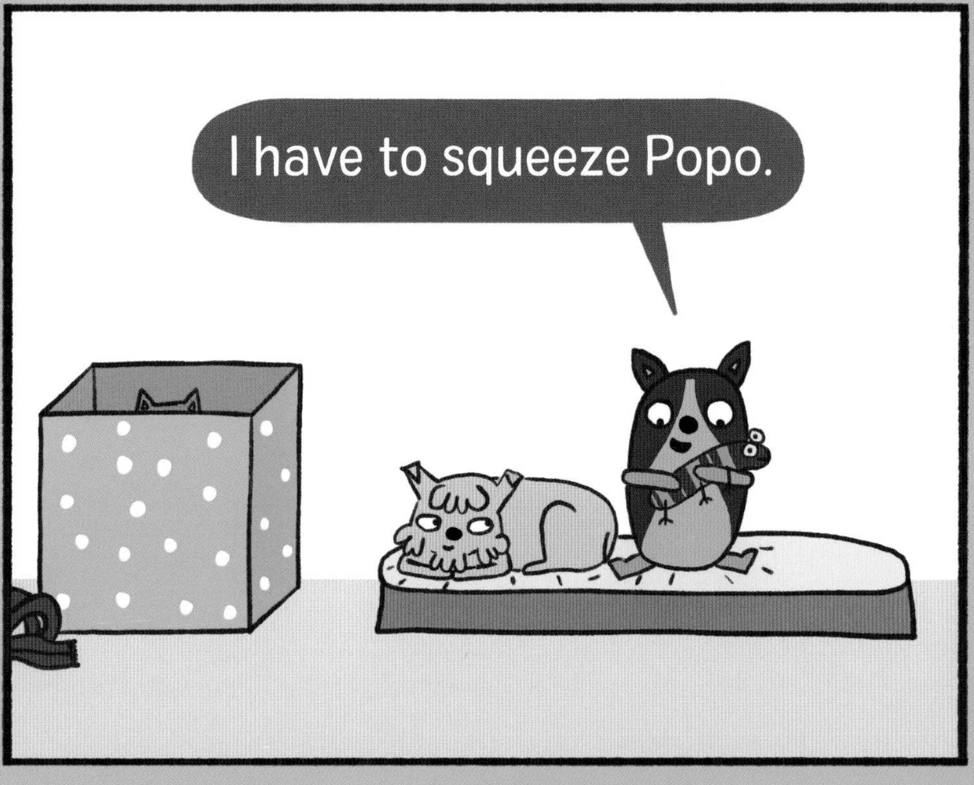
I have to squeeze Popo.

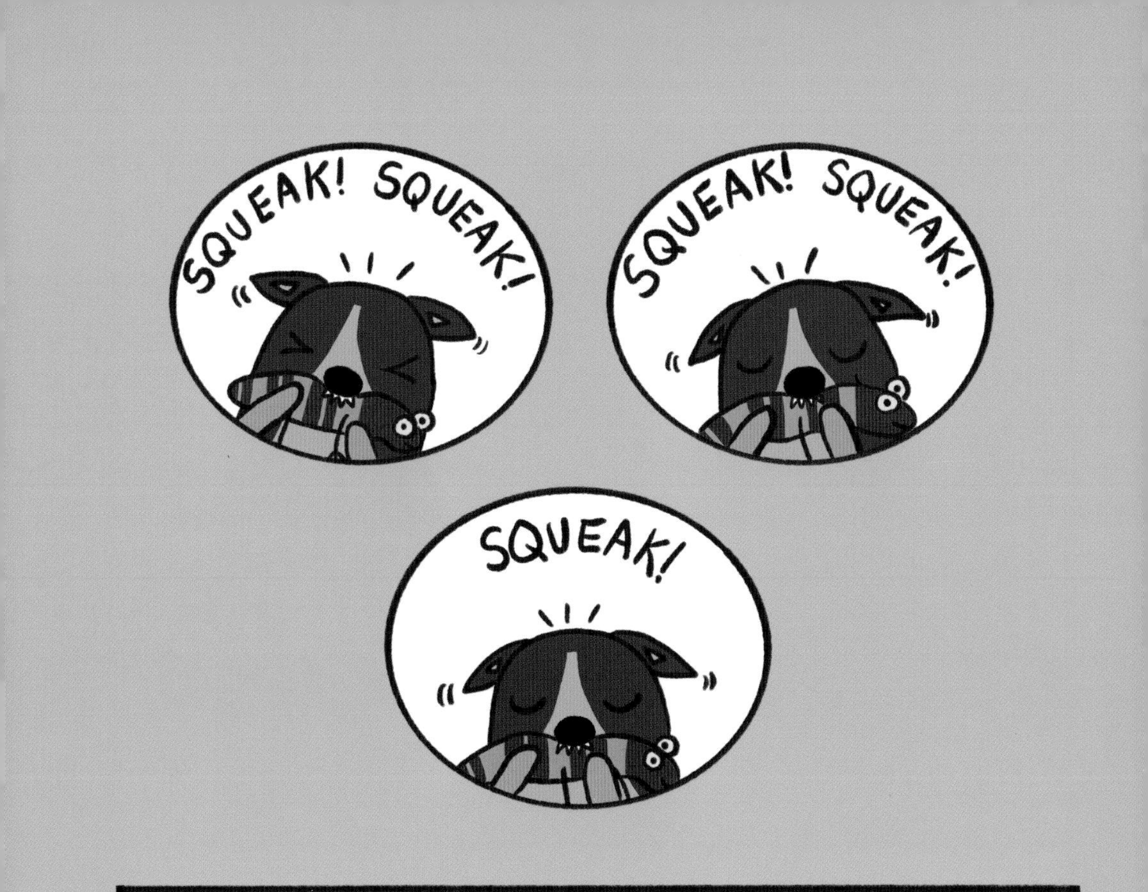
SQUEAK! SQUEAK!
SQUEAK! SQUEAK!
SQUEAK!

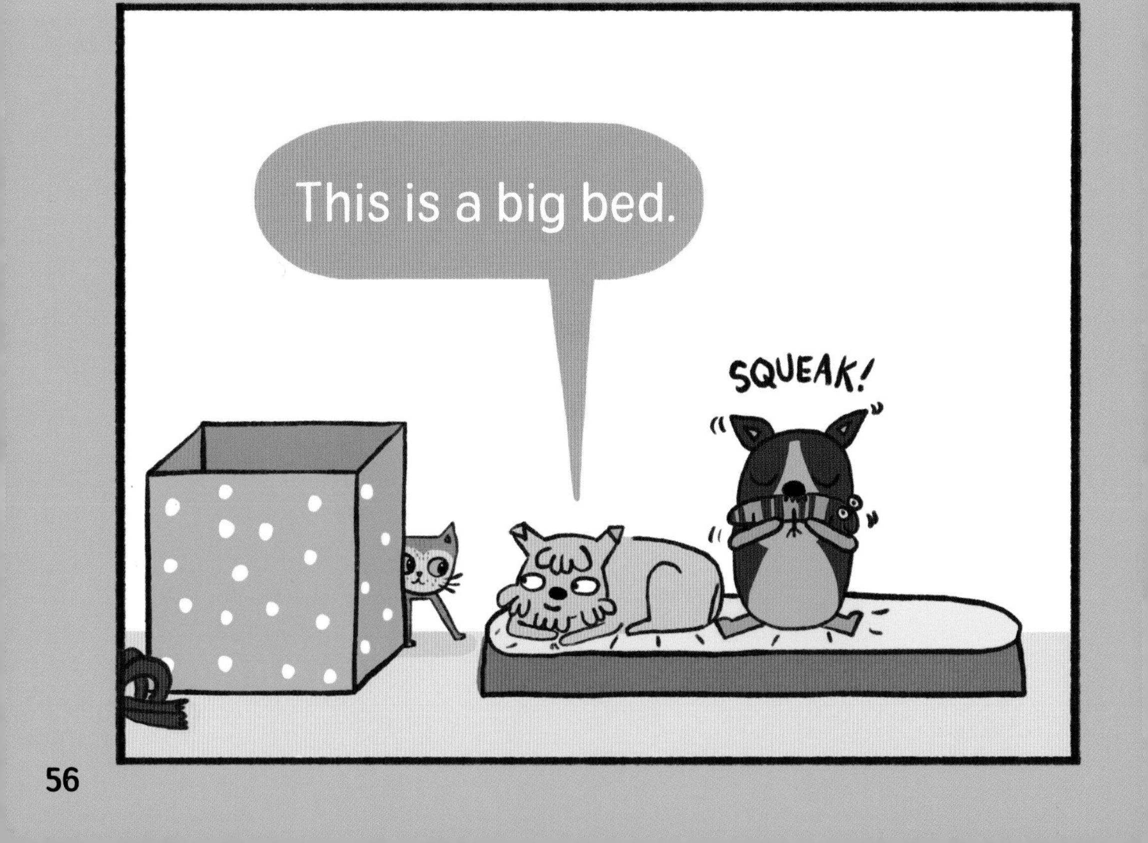
This is a big bed.
SQUEAK!

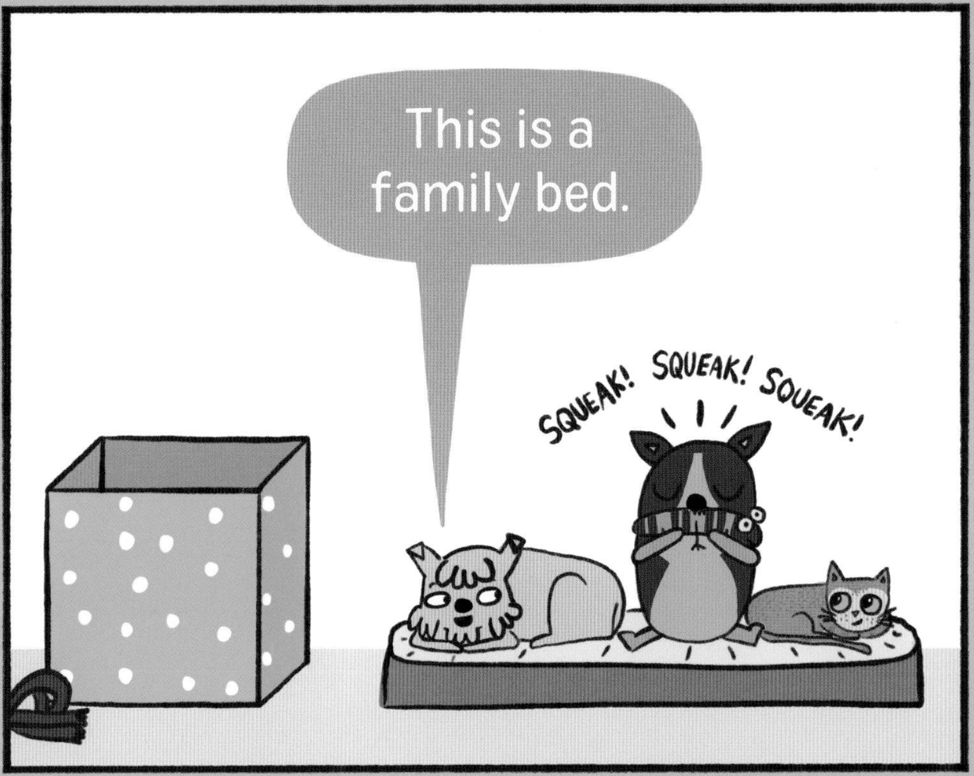
This is a family bed.
SQUEAK! SQUEAK! SQUEAK!

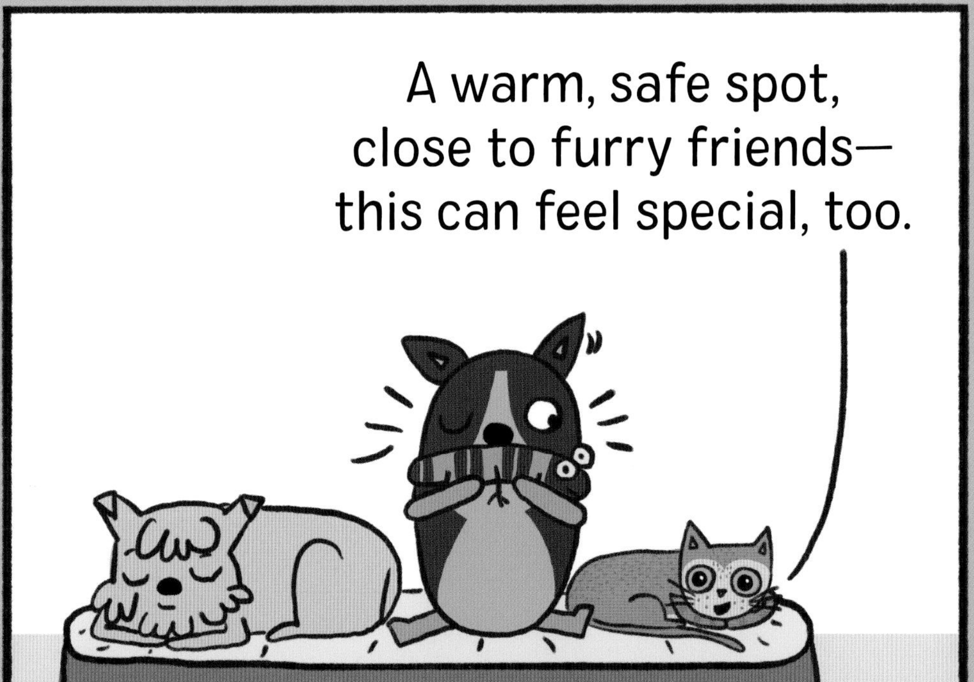
A warm, safe spot,
close to furry friends—
this can feel special, too.

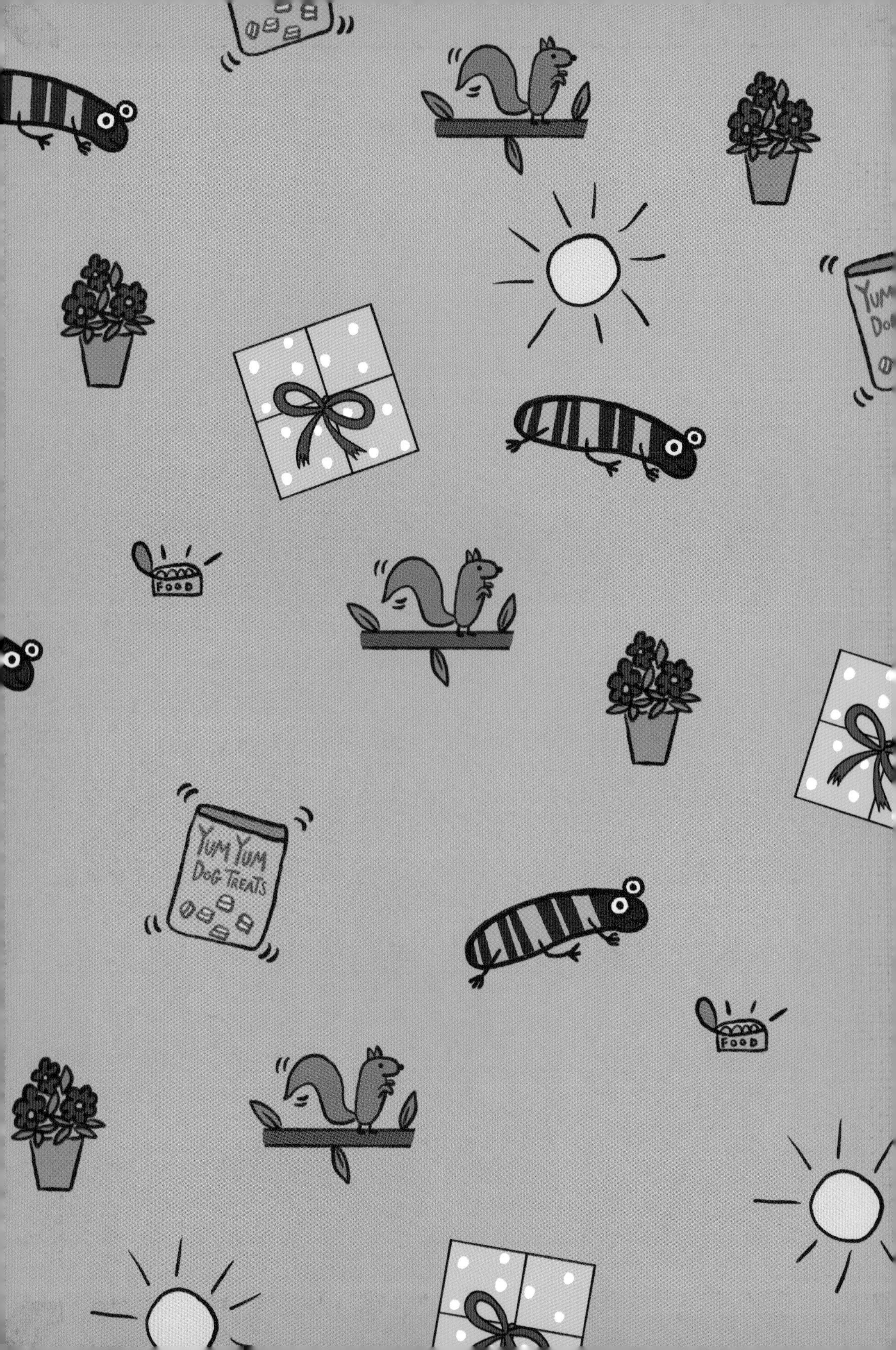
FOOD
YUM YUM
DOG TREATS
FOOD